SILVER BELLS
and
SECRETS

ALSO BY LAURA ROLLINS

Daughters of Courage
The Audacious Miss Eliza
The Determined Miss Rachel
The Fearless Miss Dinah
The Tenacious Lady Blackmore (coming Spring 2022)

A Dickens of a Christmas
The Hope of Christmas Past
The Joy of Christmas Present
The Peace of Christmas Yet to Come

Lockhart Regency Romance
Courting Miss Penelope--available at www.LauraRollins.com
Wager for a Lady's Hand
Lily for my Enemy
A Heart in the Balance
A Farewell Kiss
A Well-Kept Promise

Twelfth Night Novellas
Silver Bells and Secrets
Sugar Plums and Scandal (coming Christmas 2022)

Stand Alone Regency Romances
A Wish for Father Christmas (part of A Christmas Match series)

SILVER BELLS
and
SECRETS

TWELFTH NIGHT NOVELLA

LAURA ROLLINS

To Kendra,
One of the smartest and kindest people I know

ONE

OF ALL THE EARLS to hold the Weston title, Ezra was certain he was the most imbecilic of them all.

He'd called one of the women he danced with at the ball last night "pretty enough," and to her mother, he'd said, "I'd as soon dance with you as your daughter." In the moment, he'd of course meant it as a compliment. But as soon as the words left his mouth, he'd been instantly, painfully aware of how awkward and . . . easy to misunderstand they had been.

Ezra took another sip of port and leaned back in the comfortable wingback, the one that was worn in all the right places and held him just so. At least here, in his own house, sitting behind his own desk, he rarely caused insult or offense. It was rather a pity he couldn't attend balls from this position. Here, he was himself. Here, the words that left his mouth made sense and pieced themselves together without much fuss. But one step beyond these walls, it was a whole different matter.

"Hiding again?" Frances swept into the room without a knock or greeting.

Ezra eyed his sister, eight years younger than he. Her hair was perfectly set in curls and tied with ribbons, her dress had cost him heaven knew how much, and still, she didn't smile.

"Don't tell me you intend to confine me to the house all day again," she demanded more than asked.

"If you have some place else to go, I will not stop you." Though Ezra loved Frances dearly, when he'd agreed to take her and Mother to London for the Season, he hadn't realized that meant he'd actually agreed to host party after party and accept every invitation to a ball or musicale or dinner party that came their way.

Frances pursed her lips, folded her arms, and scowled at him. "You're just upset because Lady Martha preferred dancing with Lord Beckstead."

Ezra didn't dignify her comment with a response.

"It's your own fault," she continued, taking the seat across from his desk. "You just have to relax a bit while among society."

Ezra let out a snort. She had no idea how impossible that was.

Frances cast him an exasperated glare. "If you're going to give up on society, at least have the decency to do so *after* I've caught a husband."

Ezra leaned forward, placing his forearms against the desk. "I'm not giving up. I just . . . I don't find it easy to converse with strangers."

She blinked at him, no compassion in her eyes. "So improve."

He intertwined his fingers atop the desk. He hadn't truly expected her to understand.

Frances smoothed her skirt. "I believe this is the part where Father would have said, 'Of course, dearest; anything you want.'"

"Is that so?" This was how it always went. If Ezra showed any inkling of not giving Frances everything she wanted, his sister always insisted Father would have had he not passed so many years ago. As such, Ezra was bound by duty to give in—or so Frances believed.

"Yes," she continued, her pout only growing. "I'm sure he would have allowed—"

The door opened, and Frances whirled around in her seat, no doubt hoping one of the many friends she'd made in London this past year had come to visit.

Instead, it was only Adam, one of the footmen. "This morning's post just arrived, my lord."

"Very good." Ezra motioned the man forward.

Adam deposited the letters—and there were many of them—in Ezra's hand and left the room.

"How many are for me?" Frances asked eagerly.

Ezra set the letters down, ready to sort through them. But Frances's hands were faster. She reached out, spreading the thick stack across the desk, and flipped over several at once.

"Mine," she said after reading the neat script across the front. She then placed the letter directly in front of her and without caring to open it, continued to grab at another letter. "Mine." She placed it with the first. "Mine. Mine."

Ezra leaned back. "Let me know when you're finished."

She didn't bother responding but continued to gather more and more of the letters. Not that Ezra was surprised—it seemed nearly every woman in all of London believed she must write his sister at least once a fortnight or risk being cast from all good society forever.

Finally, Frances unceremoniously shoved the remaining three letters in Ezra's direction, scooped up the many others, and hurried over toward the window seat. Sitting before the warm July sunlight, she hurriedly flipped through her stack and found one to tear open and read.

Ezra shook his head. At least he'd have peace and quiet for the next few minutes while Frances devoured the letters—read in order of the sender's place among society, naturally. Frances treated her letters rather like people lining up to go into dinner at an elegant gathering. Those with the highest titles got to go first, and those with lesser connections waited until last.

Ezra laughed softly to himself and turned his own gaze to the three very thin letters left to him. Two revealed handwriting so well known to him, there was no need to open the letters and read the name at the bottom. The first was from his man of business and the second from an old friend. But the third caught his eye.

He reached for it and picked it up between two fingers. He didn't recognize the handwriting at all. More still, it looked quite feminine. Why the blazes would a woman write him?

He studied the words closer and sighed. Lowering it, but not dropping the letter completely, he stared over at Frances. "You missed one."

"Oh?" Her eyes never left the letter she was currently inhaling. "Who's it from?"

Ezra turned the letter over, but there was no name other than his sister's. He broke the seal and shook it open. His gaze jumped to the bottom. "Miss Grace Stewart," he read aloud.

Frances said nothing. Ezra lifted his eyes and looked at her over the top of the letter. All her focus was still upon the letter in her hands.

"Frances?" he asked.

"Hmm?"

He held the letter out toward her. "Miss Stewart has also written you."

"All right." She still did not look up.

Ezra waited a minute, but when his sister placed the letter she had been reading aside and took up the next one, he shook the one he held in her direction. "Frances."

"What?" Her tone was instantly high-pitched and annoyed.

"Miss Stewart has also written you."

Her gaze dropped to the floor, and she shrugged, angling away from him a bit. "And what if she has?"

Ezra's brow creased. Frances seemed not the least bit interested in reading what one of her friends had to say, which was odd in the extreme.

He thought back on the many ladies Frances had collected as friends. Had he been introduced to Miss Stewart before? No, he didn't believe so. He may not have felt comfortable speaking much around others, but he almost never forgot a name. He hadn't been introduced to her, but now that he thought about it, he was certain she'd been pointed out to him once. He'd been standing across the room at the opera. It was during intermission, and he'd gone to get refreshments for himself, Frances, and Mother. A rather pretty young lady had smiled their direction and Frances had smiled back, then identified the woman as Miss Stewart.

At the time, he'd been rather overwhelmed at being in the middle of a veritable crush, but now that he thought back on the night, it struck him as odd that Frances, for once, had not rushed off to greet an acquaintance. He leaned forward, his eyes on his sister, and tapped the letter gently against his lips. Did she not like this Miss Stewart? He'd only seen her for the briefest of moments, but there had been nothing haughty or arrogant in Miss Stewart's expression, at least not that he'd noticed.

"Then I take it," Ezra said, his words coming out slowly, "that you are not on friendly terms with Miss Stewart?"

"I didn't say that, exactly." Frances was on the last letter in her stack; she'd rushed through them far too fast to enjoy any of the carefully written words.

"Is she an unkind woman?"

Frances let out what sounded surprisingly like a snort and looked his direction for the first time in many minutes. "Why do you care?"

Ezra held up his hands. "I only want to know why this letter is not to be devoured with the rest."

"Ezra." Frances swung his direction and spoke in her "mother voice," the one she used whenever she believed he was being particularly dense and needed the most rudimentary aspects of life explained to him. "She is *Miss* Stewart. I would think the answer is obvious. Her father may be a gentleman, but there hasn't been a title in their family as far back as Alexander the Great. She was raised in the country with little or no society about. I've seen her wear the same dress two or three times at least. Her performance on the pianoforte desperately needs polishing, and her dancing is hardly graceful. She is not at all the kind of lady with whom one wishes to be associated."

Ezra was dumbfounded.

Granted, he could never be called a man of many words, but this was different. He didn't remain silent now because he was nervous or among strangers. He remained silent because he had never known his sister's vanity to extend so far.

"Are you saying," he said, "that because Miss Stewart is not likely to propel you upward among society and provide you with promising connections, you won't even take five minutes to respond to a letter from her?"

"If you care so much, why don't *you* write her?"

"What utter rot." He couldn't believe Frances was turning her nose up in such a way. "Very well." He shook the letter out again and held it open with both hands. "If you can't be bothered to read Miss Stewart's letter yourself, I shall have to read it to you."

Frances only coughed out a disbelieving chortle.

"*Lady Frances,*" Ezra began. "*It has only been a single week since I left London, and I find myself quite conflicted over being back home. I do miss you and several other ladies of our acquaintance there, but I cannot help but confess I find it a relief to be away from the crushes and ever-judgmental stares. How hard it always was to find the right thing to say, the right topic of conversation. You were always so much better at that sort of thing than I.*"

Ezra's voice slowed, the words he read aloud a surprising echo of his own thoughts and feelings.

Do you remember the evening you introduced me to Lord Brown? He lives not far from my current home, and yet, we'd never once been introduced. You were so charming and knew exactly how to keep his interest. Meanwhile, I stood by, mute and awkward. Gracious, but I felt certain you would have no interest in continuing to be my friend after that night.

Frances stood, and the subtle noise brought Ezra's head up.

"I thought you were going to read it aloud."

Had he stopped? He couldn't remember when he'd turned to reading the words silently. Only, the thoughts expressed therein felt so familiar, so much like his own. He could very easily understand how Miss Stewart would feel relief at being away from London, even if it meant more solitude.

He held Miss Stewart's letter out. "You need to answer this, Frances." Ezra may have only laid eyes on Miss Stewart once in his entire life, but the few emotions she'd openly expressed on the page were painfully familiar. Miss Stewart was lonely and had struggled to find footing among the *ton*. A kind word from Frances would go a long way in helping her feel confident enough about herself to do better next year.

Frances, however, only spread the letters in her hand and fanned herself with them. "Dear me, if only I could. But I am so busy answering all of these."

"I'm not saying you have to invite her to live with us. Only write her back."

"Because we both came out during the same Season? So I must now be her dearest friend forever?" She batted her lashes. "What a quaint notion." She turned her back to him.

"Frances," Ezra called, but she didn't spare him a second glance as she passed out of the room.

He'd rather been wondering if Mother wasn't spoiling Frances too much, if *he* allowed it too often. Apparently, he should have stopped wondering and started changing things long ago. His gaze dropped to the letter still in his hand. He would speak to Mother about Frances later. For now, what was to be done about Miss Stewart? The rest of her letter—which he was fully aware he should not be reading but couldn't resist regardless—was more of the same. Though she never came right out and said she was unhappy and worried she'd never find her place among society, it was all there, nonetheless.

After he finished the short letter, Ezra found himself reading it a second time, and then a third. The letter was sweet, and yet it also tugged at his heart. This young woman clearly needed a friend. His gaze fell to the ink pot and extra foolscap he kept on hand to write his own letters. What was the chance he could convince Frances to write Miss Stewart back? Poor, at best.

Which was horribly sad. Because it was clear that Miss Stewart needed a response. She needed to know that *someone* she met in London had noticed she'd left, cared she was gone, and had thought of her while she was away. It wouldn't have to be much. But Ezra knew the power of a short, kind word at just the right time.

He placed Miss Stewart's letter down, his hand cupping his chin and mouth. He wasn't particularly gifted at speaking to strangers, but that changed when it came time to write down his thoughts. He could more easily express himself in writing than he ever could while speaking.

Did he dare though?

Frances had suggested the very thing he was thinking now, but only in jest. He himself had called the notion "utter rot." Gentlemen did not write ladies they were not connected to, either as a brother, father, or intended. Only a lady could write another lady.

Which was why he deeply wished he could get Frances to write the letter.

Then again . . . Miss Stewart didn't have to know it *wasn't* Frances who'd written her back. It wasn't as though Miss Stewart had received letters from Frances in the past and so would know what her handwriting looked like. He could always express a thoughtful word and then sign it with his sister's name. No one would be hurt by the small untruth, and indeed a great deal of good would probably come from it.

Blast, what was he thinking? Ezra ran a hand through his hair. He was completely insane to even consider the notion.

And yet . . .

. . . Miss Stewart *did* deserve a letter back. And Frances wasn't going to be writing one herself . . .

Miss Grace Stewart nearly skipped across the room when the butler informed her that she'd received a letter. She'd written ever so many the week before last, and not a single lady of her acquaintance had yet to write back. Her London Season had been painfully awkward and lonely. But this one letter, this single response, meant it hadn't been for naught.

She had at least one friend. If that's all she could claim after an eternity of uncomfortable dinner parties and stumbling during musicales, then so be it. This lady would no doubt be her dearest friend for life.

Grace took the letter, hungrily taking in every detail. Most important, though, was the signature at the bottom. To her joy, her new and most blessed friend was Lady Frances Stanhope.

TWO

FIVE MONTHS LATER

Ezra's head bobbed with the roll of the carriage, his thoughts and emotions a veritable storm inside him. How the blazes had he gotten himself into this mess? It had only been a letter or two. *Or a dozen.* Blast it all. Surely the penned word had never before caused so much trouble.

Ezra reached for the curtain and drew it back to peer through the glass window. Snow fell lightly around them. Blessedly, not enough to cause problems for his journey. It was the first thing that had gone right since a fortnight ago.

The day he had received Miss Grace Stewart's most recent letter.

I must confess, she'd written, *that I find myself quite taken with Lord Brown. Do I deceive myself in the hopes that he quite fancies me as well? He has invited me and my parents to his house for Christmas. Surely that must mean something.*

Mean something it most certainly had.

It meant Ezra had, that very hour, written to Lord Brown's mother, Lady Brown, and all but begged to be numbered among the party. It meant that Ezra had worked alongside his valet and two footmen veritably throwing his jackets and breeches into a trunk in the effort to arrive at Bridgecross Manor as soon after Grace as possible.

Just over the horizon, he caught sight of the towering home which was his destination. Ezra let the curtain drop back down again. Never had a few written words struck him so forcibly. He curled a hand into a fist, his gloved fingers pressing tightly against his palm.

Grace was taken with Lord Brown. She believed him to be taken with her.

The news was not just unpleasant; it had brought with it a sickening, staggering, stunning revelation. Indeed, it was a most unwelcome truth. A horrid realization.

The carriage rolled to a stop, Ezra rocking forward with it. There was the sound of a footman scurrying forward, the steps being lowered, the door opening. Cold winter wind blew into the carriage which had long since grown warm from all his restless shifting about. The footman bowed low, waiting for him to exit. Ezra hesitated.

His eyes moved over the stately manor. Was she here already?

He'd only once laid eyes on Grace, and to his dismay, the memory of her was vague. Of course, he'd happened to see her across the room at the opera *before* he'd first written her. If he'd known then what utter foolish events would entwine them together, he would have taken more note of her. As it was, he remembered her being petite—possibly—with dark hair—he believed—and with an easy smile—though that last part might have been his imagination because her letters were of a generally positive nature.

The footman outside still bowed. Ezra scolded himself for leaving the man waiting.

He stepped down out of the carriage and hurried up the steps before he could hesitate again. The door was opened to him at once. An elderly man dressed in the fashion of a butler bowed deeply before him, much as the footman had. Whatever else Ezra may have learned about Lord Brown, he had to admit the man knew how to impress upon his staff the importance of offering a warm welcome to guests.

"Welcome, Lord Weston," the butler intoned. "His lordship is quite happy you have chosen to join us this holiday season."

"Thank you," Ezra said, his gaze traveling the full distance of the entryway. It was made up of the usual; pictures and sconces decorated the walls, and fresh flowers, no doubt from a local hothouse, adorned the tables. He didn't even bother taking in the floor. What else could he notice except that what *wasn't* present was a petite woman with dark hair.

"Have most of the guests already arrived?" Ezra asked, slipping off his greatcoat.

"Yes, my lord," the butler said, taking the coat, Ezra's hat, and his thick winter gloves. "You are the last."

No surprise there. His plans had been made rather last minute.

"And are they all visiting in a parlor or drawing room?"

The butler's right eyebrow ticked up ever so briefly—the only indication he was surprised at being asked so many pointed questions. "Those that arrived today are up in their rooms resting from their travels. But a few others are in the East Drawing Room. Would you care for me to show you to your bedchamber so you might freshen up?"

"Later." Ezra waved away the offer. "Just point me in the direction of the East Drawing Room."

"Very good, my lord. If you would follow me."

Ezra clasped his hands behind his back as he followed the butler up a flight of stairs and down the corridor. His fingers fidgeted as they'd been doing all day, and it grew increasingly difficult not to let loose, skip ahead of the butler, and charge into the drawing room unannounced. Ezra ground his jaw, willing his nerves to calm down. He was a grown man acting like a little boy on the first day of school holiday. This was ridiculous.

The butler opened the drawing room door and stepped inside to announce Ezra's arrival.

Ezra moved into the room. His gaze found Miss Stewart immediately. She sat on a settee halfway across the room. Her hair was not quite so dark as he'd remembered, and since she was sitting, he couldn't fully judge if she was shorter or taller than he'd imagined. But her smile was there, just as he'd believed it would be. She laughed lightly, the sound sending butterflies skittering about his insides and warming his entire being.

He'd never heard her voice. Not once.

He'd read her words, knew her thoughts, had learned much about her past and her hopes for the future. But he'd never once heard her voice.

Ezra let out a long slow breath. He had to pull himself together. Frances was always impressing upon him the importance of first impressions. Should he smile broadly at her? Offer her a most elegant bow? Frances also said that eyes could express much. Was there a look that said *I know we've never met, but we've actually been writing one another for over five months now, though I've been using my sister's name and you've no doubt believed you were writing another woman and not her brother at all, but it's still me; the one who knows you love to embroider images of the places you knew as a child, who knows you read the same lines of poetry over and over again for the love of them, and who knows you spend hours during the summer out on your balcony, wishing on every falling star you see; the one who knows you hate large crushes, who knows your toes hurt when they get too cold, and knows you are truly scared of growing old alone.*

No. Surely there was no look in all the word that could convey even half of that.

Grace was sitting beside their host, and she laughed again at something he said. Ezra's stomach was quickly growing heavy. Lord Brown was well known among Town for his flirting ways. Did Grace know that a man such as he might very well pay a lady attentions he never intended to make good on? Ezra's hands curling back into fists.

Lady Brown reached his side and greeted him.

Ezra returned a half-hearted thanks for being allowed to join them for the Christmas house party. Even as the older woman explained on and on about their surprise at his sudden wish to join them and then quickly moved on to pointing out the various other guests, Ezra's mind never left Grace.

What a mess he'd made for himself. The horrid truth he'd been wrestling with since he'd read her last letter a fortnight ago stood before him now, immovable and undeniable.

The truth was, Ezra had never been properly introduced to Grace. He could not walk over to her, greet her, sit down to a conversation with her. He could not ask her what she'd learned most recently in her French lessons, which she very much enjoyed. He could not inform her of his most recent journey to Hampshire, though she'd sounded quite eager to hear about it in her last letter.

The truth was, Ezra was a stranger to Grace. Once the dowager led him toward her, there would be no spark of recognition in her eyes, no barely hidden smile at her joy in seeing him. There would be nothing but hope on his part and disinterest on hers.

The truth—that horrid realization—was that Ezra was wholly, completely, unequivocally in love with a woman who didn't even know his face.

THREE

GRACE LAUGHED AGAIN AS Lord Brown continued his rant on the horrors of his most recent trip to a local haberdashery.

"The belt clashed with the buttons like you couldn't imagine," he said, barely containing his own laugh. "And yet, the old man continued to push the belt at me, like I was a fool for not wanting it."

"Come now, Lord Brown," Grace said, her fingers hovering over her lips in case they were needed to stop an unseemly burst of giggles. "Surely he only meant to please you."

Lord Brown cast his eyes upward. "Gracious knows what he would have thrown at me if he'd been wanting to scare me off."

"Don't be so cruel," Grace continued, still trying hard not to laugh.

He caught her eyes suddenly, his mirth momentarily calming. "Your desire to believe the best in the shopkeeper does you credit, Miss Stewart."

Grace's face heated, and she looked down. How the heavens had orchestrated such a blessing as Lord Brown's pointed attention, she would never know. She was the daughter of a gentleman, but not one who was titled. She was from the country, had only been to Town for the first time this year, and was in no way well connected. And yet, here she sat, laughing with Lord Brown, welcomed at his home until Twelfth Night, nearly three weeks hence. If she'd known this blessing had only been around the corner, this past year would not have been quite so miserable. At least she'd had Lady Frances's letters—the only bright spot in an otherwise wretched, lonely Season.

As Grace lifted her head once more, her gaze caught on a man standing near the door, Lady Brown at his side. She'd been vaguely aware of when he'd entered the room and been announced. But she'd been so caught up in Lord Brown's tale, she hadn't spared the gentleman a second thought. Now that she did think on it, it had been rather rude of Lord Brown not to acknowledge the arrival of another guest. He'd probably been too engrossed in his own tale as well.

Or perhaps too diverted by the woman he was speaking with?

Gracious, no. Grace's face warmed once more. She believed, or rather sincerely hoped, that Lord Brown was beginning to feel something for her. But she was far from the only eligible young woman invited to the Christmas house party. Though they had spoken to one another often since she'd arrived the day before, he hadn't exactly singled her out for all his attentions.

"Now," Lord Brown said, pulling her thoughts back to him, as he always did whenever he opened his mouth or even walked into a room. "Guess what we shall be eating tonight. I am sure you will be quite delighted once you find out."

Grace pinched her lips in thought. "Mutton?"

Lord Brown shook his head.

"Lamb?" Though Grace's head was full of foods that might be served that evening, she couldn't help but feel her gaze drawn back toward the gentleman near the door.

He was watching her. It seemed evident that he was in conversation with the dowager, and yet his eyes remained on Grace.

"Cooked carrots?" Grace heard herself say. Who was the gentleman who stared so unceasingly? Had her skirts hiked up around her ankles again? She did very much appreciate the new silk dresses her parents had purchased for this holiday visit, and the extra thick stockings were a warm indulgence to help prevent her toes from getting too cold. But the two clothing items, while both fine in quality and appearance and worthy of Grace's sincere appreciation, did not appreciate one another. They seemed to almost bicker in the way they caught time and again.

"I am not speaking of the main course," Lord Brown said. "I mean dessert."

"Oh?" Grace forced her gaze back to Lord Brown and smiled at him, all the while subtly reaching for her skirt and fluffing it back out so it would surely fall to the floor without causing her more grief. "Plum pudding, then?"

"Mother insists we save that for Christmas Day. Guess again."

"You know quite a bit about what we will be eating and when, my lord," Grace said. The gentleman by the door was *still* looking over at her. Grace hazarded a glance his way. He wasn't looking at her skirt, however, so perhaps that hadn't been the issue at all. Instead, he was focused on her face, his gaze meeting hers.

There was something in his expression . . . but what, exactly, Grace couldn't say.

"Miss Stewart?" Lord Brown leaned forward, catching her gaze once more.

"Sorry." Grace shook herself. Had Lord Brown been speaking?

"Do you not agree that desserts are worth knowing about so one might anticipate them?"

Right. Grace nodded quickly in agreement. She'd asked why he knew so much about what they would eat. That, and she was trying to guess tonight's dessert. Grace scrambled to think of another sweet. "Honey cake?"

"The very thing. How clever of you."

Grace dropped her gaze yet again, hoping to hide another blush. But despite Lord Brown's praise, she couldn't shake her awareness of the other gentleman. The dowager motioned toward one side of the room, and she and the gentleman began walking that way. No doubt she intended to introduce him to the other guests.

The pause in her conversation with Lord Brown had grown into a decided lull, and Grace spoke the first thing that came to mind. "I do adore honey cake." The last thing she wanted was for Lord Brown to think she didn't enjoy his company, and yet, she was suddenly struggling to find things to say. Perhaps she ought to encourage him to take over the conversation once more. "Tell me, what else will we be enjoying tonight?"

Lord Brown delved into a long list of various foods. The baron and the dowager certainly knew how to host a festive Christmas— and apparently Lord Brown believed *all* types of foods should be anticipated well in advance.

As Lord Brown spoke, Grace kept her eyes on him, but her mind followed the dowager and the gentleman at her side. If she wasn't wrong, the gentleman continued to look over at her often. Had she something on her face? A lock of curl jutting out from her coiffure?

Hoping not to draw much attention to herself, Grace carefully patted down her hair. Nothing seemed out of place. She brushed a hand over her cheek. It had been at least three hours since she'd last eaten. Suppose she'd had some bit of food left on her face all this time? She would be mortified. But her fingers came away clean.

"Miss Stewart."

Grace turned and found the dowager and the gentleman already upon her.

"May I make you known to the Earl of Weston?"

He was an earl? Good heavens. No doubt a man of his standing would find much fault in someone such as herself. Still, she tipped her head in agreement.

"Lord Weston," the dowager continued, "this is Miss Stewart. She and her parents will be with us the entire party, though Mr. and Mrs. Stewart are currently upstairs. I do believe you will find them quite pleasant when you make their acquaintance. And of course you know my son, Lord Brown."

The man in question stood, extending his arm to Lord Weston. "Do forgive my lapse in etiquette. I'm afraid I was rather busy speaking with the lovely Miss Stewart and did not even realize you'd arrived."

Lovely? Did he truly believe she was lovely?

Save her father, never had a man paid her so much attention or spoken so well of her. Despite her hesitance to accept them, her heart had been keeping careful count of every compliment to come from Lord Brown. He was up to three now—three clearly flattering compliments—and Grace suddenly wondered if her hopes would be realized after all.

"Miss Stewart," Lord Weston said, his voice low and smooth. "It is an honor to meet you at last."

"At last, my lord?" She couldn't fathom what he meant. Was he known to her father? Or an uncle, perhaps?

"I believe you and my sister met in London during the summer. Lady Frances Stanhope."

"Oh, of course." Grace knew the words were too loud the moment she'd said them. She tried to tone down her voice, but it was rather hard when speaking of someone as kind and good as Lady Frances.

"Your sister has become my dearest friend." Grace turned toward Lord Brown and the dowager. "Lady Frances and I write one another at least once a week. Nothing brightens my day like receiving a letter from her."

Grace glanced over at Lord Weston. His smile had turned tight. If she wasn't mistaken, he was rather grinding his teeth, the tension showing along his jaw and down his neck. Despite all that, he was quite handsome. Sandy hair fell about his face. His jaw was well defined, though that could just be the tension. He had a straight nose and light blue eyes. A beautiful shade of blue, at that. Exactly the color she would use to embroider a spring sky or a robin's egg.

Still, there was a tightness to his expression. It seemed as though he held something back—as though he'd already judged her unequal to his trust and confidence. Unequal to *him*. He was an earl after all, and very probably considered her a country bumkin.

He probably didn't approve of his sister writing her. Well, it didn't matter. She wasn't about to give up her friend for anyone.

Grace turned back to Lord Brown. "I know of no one as kind-hearted and gracious as Lady Frances." She purposely did not look at Lady Frances's brother as she spoke the words. Let him look down on her if he must; she would stand by his sister's side regardless.

"I met Lady Frances a few times in London," Lord Brown said, his brow creasing. "I must confess, I rather find it surprising to hear you consider her such a good friend."

"Why is that?" Grace asked.

"Only, the two of you are so different."

"At first, I felt the same. But on closer acquaintance, I found she and I had many things in common." She'd not considered Lady Frances overly much, until one afternoon, in a fit of complete loneliness, Grace had written nearly everyone she'd met in London, praying desperately that *someone* would care to continue an acquaintance with her enough to write back. Lady Frances had. More still, it had been a most warm and encouraging letter. So Grace had written her yet again, and Lady Frances had replied, and on and on until now they wrote each other about everything.

"Some people," Grace said, "are perhaps not so much themselves among society as they are when they can write down their thoughts and reflections." Grace often felt that way herself. Though she enjoyed company—not crushes, but pleasant conversations—she still often felt she opened up more easily when writing than when talking.

"I suppose that may be true," Lord Brown said, tipping his head to the side as though carefully mulling over what she'd said.

"Come, Lord Weston," the dowager said, breaking into the conversation once more. "I shall introduce you to Lord and Lady Thompson next."

Lord Weston seemed to hesitate, casting Grace yet another look— another that felt as though it meant . . . *more*. He seemed to be trying to communicate something to her, yet she couldn't figure out what it was.

The dowager looped her arm around his and all but pulled him away. Grace watched him leave.

"Do you know Lord Weston well?" she found herself asking after he and the dowager were out of ear shot.

Lord Brown shrugged. "Not overly. But he personally requested to be included on the guest list, and I knew better than to turn down an earl."

"How very strange."

Lord Brown nodded. "My impression of him in Town was that he is a quiet sort. Keeps to himself. Perhaps he is like you were saying and is one of those individuals who opens up more easily in writing than in company."

"He is Lady Frances's brother, so perhaps they are both of that nature."

Lord Weston glanced over his shoulder, and his gaze caught hers yet again.

A zip of pure heat burst through her, as though lightning had struck her heart. Grace leaned back and blinked several times. Never had a glance from *anyone* caused such a reaction inside her.

"Are you all right, Miss Stewart?" Lord Brown asked.

Grace forced her lips upward and into something she hoped looked like a smile. "Yes, my lord. I am quite well. Now, I believe you were telling me about tonight's dinner before we were interrupted."

"Ah, yes. The potatoes will be absolute perfection, you can count on that."

As Lord Brown dove back into his monologue about that evening's meal, Grace utterly refused to give Lord Weston another glance. She was here to enjoy her Christmas after a trying year. She was here to make friends and hope for less harshly judgmental connections. She was here to encourage the man sitting beside her, as she found him to be the most pleasing man of her acquaintance.

No one and nothing, not even the Earl of Weston, was going to ruin Christmas for her.

FOUR

THE DOWAGER OPENED THE double doors and swept into the room ahead of the ladies. "And this is our music room," she announced. "I am hoping we can depend on each of you to perform during the small musicale I have planned for next week."

Grace took in the room. Light yellow curtains framed the windows along one wall. Her eyes were drawn to them immediately as they were her favorite shade. There was a pianoforte nearest them, and beside that instrument, a small table with a lovely bust statue. There weren't many chairs in the room, but most likely the staff would bring more in on the night of the musicale.

"What a charming space," Lady Augusta said from beside Grace. The woman's parents, Lord and Lady Honeyfield, had shown themselves thus far to be kind and considerate guests. Their daughter equally so. "I think all would enjoy a musicale in such a delightful room."

"I am quite the proficient on the pianoforte," Lady Katherine said, her pitch as high and screeching as ever. "I would be happy to close the night out for us all." She turned toward Grace and Lady Augusta. "I believe that would allow everyone to end their evening most happily entertained."

Grace only blinked in response—she never would have dared be so bold herself. To *request* to be the final performer? Heavens, it was nearly a declaration of one's self as the absolute best of them all. Not that Grace doubted Lady Katherine would outshine her. Grace was not so gifted on the pianoforte.

If only she were permitted to showcase a pillow she'd embroidered, that would be a different story altogether.

Lady Brown looped a hand around Lady Katherine's arm. "Wonderful." She turned toward Grace and Lady Augusta. "And may we count on the both of you as well?"

Lady Augusta was still eying the room. "I have a song or two I feel confident enough to perform."

The dowager's gaze rested on Grace, clearly waiting for her agreement as well.

"Might I perform on the harp instead of the pianoforte?" She was not quite as clumsy on that instrument.

Lady Brown's smile faltered. "I am sorry; we don't have a harp here at Bridgecross."

That was unfortunate.

Lady Brown hurried on, placing a hand on Grace's arm. "But surely you know at least one song you might perform for us? I know we would all dearly love to hear you."

Grace didn't feel she could tell her hostess no, and there was one song she could perform adequately enough.

"If you wish it," Grace said, trying to keep her tone optimistic. "But I'll warn you it is very simple indeed."

"Splendid," Lady Brown said, turning back to the room as a whole.

Grace didn't miss the slight uptick of Lady Katherine's eyebrow. It was quite possible the other young woman had heard tales of Grace's struggles on the pianoforte from earlier that year. Ah, well, if she had, there was nothing Grace could do about it now. Still, she wished Lady Frances was here. Having at least one friend in the audience would make such a difference.

"I do hope you ladies know how much I appreciate it," Lady Brown continued, leading them further into the room and toward a door on the opposite side. "I know this isn't a large house party, but it is still rather a strain always coming up with something to entertain everyone."

Lady Katherine squeezed Lady Brown's arm. "You can count on me to help in any way possible."

"Thank you, dear."

Grace fell into step behind Lady Brown, her gaze moving over the room as they walked. It was most elegant indeed. Far superior to even the finest room in the home where she had grown up. What must it have been like for Lord Brown to be raised among such luxury?

"I feel a little bad for Lady Brown," Lady Augusta said, stepping up beside Grace. "I think she's still a bit rattled to find herself hosting an uneven party."

Grace tore her gaze away from the damask curtains. "What do you mean?"

"Only, now that Lord Weston has secured himself an invitation last minute, there are three young women and *four* eligible men."

Grace hadn't really done the math. "Yes, but this is proving a small, intimate gathering. Do you truly think she's so put out by one additional gentleman?"

"Only consider the parents. You have both your father and mother here, as do I. Between them, they are even. Then Lady Brown invited one other widow, Lady Parsons, and two widowers, Lord Clark and Mr. Ridlington."

That *was* remarkably even. "And the young people would have been even as well. You, myself, and Lady Katherine; then Lord Brown, Mr. Banfield, and Lord Andrews." Such things were considered excessively important among the *ton*. What a chit Grace had been for not realizing the discrepancy before now.

Lady Augusta nodded as they passed back out of the music room and into the corridor once more. "Exactly. Not only that, but now she's hosting an *earl*. No wonder she's a bit . . ."

"Rattled," Grace added.

Lady Augusta nodded again, but then she smiled and leaned in closer to Grace. "Not that *I* mind having an additional eligible gentleman around the house over Christmas." She laughed lightly. "It'll make everything much more interesting, don't you think?"

Grace couldn't stop the laugh that bubbled up. "Don't be wicked."

"Oh, I don't intend to do anything truly naughty. But then again . . ." Lady Augusta's smile only grew as she cast her gaze heavenward. "If certain opportunities present themselves, and there happens to be some obliging mistletoe nearby . . ." She let her sentence dangle, giggling instead of finishing.

"Gracious, do promise me—"

Lady Augusta reached out suddenly, taking hold of Grace's arm and stopping her short. It wasn't until that moment that Grace realized someone was standing directly in front of her, as her thoughts had been so fully on Lady Augusta's diverting conversation.

Grace turned and found herself nearly toe to toe with Lord Weston—the earl who thought her too beneath his sister to even write her letters.

He appeared to be trying to smile, but it was clearly forced. No doubt he was hoping to put on a good face while they were both guests at the same house party.

"Good evening, my lord," Grace and Lady Augusta intoned almost simultaneously, even as they both offered him a short curtsy.

Lord Weston bent at the waist in a slight bow, which only brought him that much closer to Grace. An unexpected flurry of nerves coursed through Grace at his nearness. She'd met a few viscounts and barons during her London Season that year, but she could not boast meeting a single earl. No doubt, meeting a gentleman so far above one's own station was bound to make one a bit lightheaded and fluttery all over.

"Have you been enjoying yourself today?" Lady Augusta spoke up in the silence that was quickly growing awkward.

"I have," he said. Good heavens, but he had a low voice. It rumbled with every word. Did the earl sing? Grace could only imagine that if he did, it would be deep and melodious.

Deep and entrancing as his voice was, however, he didn't seem overly inclined to use it, as he said no more.

Once more, silence fell around them.

Grace glanced from him to the empty corridor around them. Apparently, she and Lady Augusta had lagged too far behind Lady Brown and Lady Katherine, as the women were nowhere in sight. It was up to them to make conversation . . . and Grace hadn't the first idea what to say to an earl.

"Lady Brown was giving us a tour of the house," Lady Augusta said, once more rescuing them all from awkwardness.

Lord Weston dipped his head. "How nice."

And . . . that was all.

Oh dear, the air around them was quickly growing as stiff as Cook's overdone pheasant. Lady Augusta had spoken up twice now; surely it was Grace's turn.

"Have you seen the music room?" Not exactly conversation to inspire and divert, but it was something.

Lord Weston turned slightly, facing her more fully. "I have, thank you. I found it to be a lovely room."

"So did I," Grace said. "It's bright and warm."

"I particularly like the height of the room," he continued. "It makes one think music would reverberate most enjoyably around the room. Did you notice the curtains?"

"Yes, I certainly did. Jonquil yellow is a favorite color of mine."

His smile softened. "I thought you might like them." And he was giving her *that look* again. The one that rested on her as though he saw no one else. As though nothing else was happening around them. It was the same look he had given her when he'd first arrived at Bridgecross Manor yesterday. Grace was equally at a loss as to why he was looking at her thusly now as she'd been then.

Lady Augusta, who'd been silent for several minutes now, spoke up then. "Would you care to join us, Lord Weston? I believe I saw Lady Brown and Lady Katherine step into the next room. If we hurry, I'm sure we can catch up."

He seemed to hesitate but only for a moment. "I would be delighted."

Much to Grace's surprise, he fell into step beside her instead of beside Lady Augusta. This placed Grace between them. It was strange to physically be in the center of things. All Season long, she'd always found herself standing along the edges of most conversations. Always just on the outside, feeling like a stranger looking in.

But as the three of them moved toward the next room, Grace had to admit she didn't feel like the unwanted country mouse everyone tolerated if only to make themselves look gracious. As the conversation moved on to most loved songs, Grace learned that Lady Augusta shared her love of Mozart. When it comfortably changed to a discussion of Vienna, Grace found that Lord Weston had, like herself, long wished to travel abroad.

Perhaps it was just a bit of Christmas magic, but for the first time in longer than she could remember, Grace felt wanted and a bit like she belonged.

FIVE

EZRA SIPPED AT HIS soup, but his gaze hardly left Grace as he did. This was the third dinner they'd all enjoyed at Bridgecross Manor, and the third time he'd failed to find a seat next to her. The first night, he'd been speaking with Lady Augusta and her parents when dinner had been announced and so had walked in with them. To do otherwise would have appeared rude, or so he told himself. It had nothing to do with the fact that merely thinking of walking across the room, striking up a conversation with Grace, and then asking if she might walk in with him sent his heart skittering about his chest in a very painful way. After all, he hated to appear too forward, too overbearing. Grace was still unaware that *he'd* been writing her these past many months. She must have enjoyed his letters, or she would not have written back such personal replies each time. If only he could get her to see some of that same friendship she'd found in their correspondence, perhaps she wouldn't curse him to Hades when he finally told her the truth.

Gads, but he hoped she wouldn't. He'd do anything for a chance at a permanent place in Grace Stewart's life.

Both last night and again tonight, Lady Katherine had been too close for him to extricate himself from her company when dinner had been called. At least in the past he'd been able to find a seat close enough to Grace to listen in on her soft voice. Tonight, she was halfway down the table. He could see her smiling at Lord Brown, but that was all. And it hardly put his mind at ease.

"Excellent potato soup, is it not?" asked Lord Andrews, a baron of about Ezra's same age.

"Quite good," Ezra said, giving the man no more than a cursory glance.

Lord Andrews chuckled, putting his spoon down and pushing his empty bowl away slightly. "The soup is white, my lord, not potato, and you are clearly besotted."

Ezra dropped his gaze to the bowl before him. White soup, just as Lord Andrews had said. Not a lump of potato anywhere.

Lord Andrews slapped him on the back. "Never fear. There's nothing wrong with being enchanted by a pair of fine eyes. Heaven knows it happens to all us blundering mortal men now and again."

Ezra placed his spoon down. "Perhaps, but I was rather hoping not to make a fool of myself over it." Let Lord Andrews think this was only a moment of bewitchment, one that would likely pass once the Christmas holiday was over. The man need never know Ezra was wholeheartedly lost to Grace or that he was convinced no amount of time passing would ever prove enough to make him forget her.

"Then stop looking her direction."

Ezra nodded. He was going about this all wrong. He knew he was. If only he could speak with her. But such an opportunity had only availed itself twice in the past three days. Yesterday, they'd toured the house together. While he enjoyed the few minutes they'd shared in the beginning, once Lady Katherine had caught sight of him walking beside Grace, she'd latched onto him and hadn't allowed him a moment of rest. Earlier today, he'd come across her as she'd been leaving the library with two books hugged close to herself.

They'd spoken of their mutual love of Byron. She'd even made him laugh as she'd described her father's reaction the first time he'd picked up a book of his poems. The way she imitated his face scrunching up, half in confusion, half in revulsion . . . it had been a perfect moment.

Until Lord Brown had rounded the corner and ruined everything.

"You know," Lord Andrews said, leaning toward him and keeping his voice low enough that only Ezra would hear even as a manservant took away their soup. "I have noticed that Lady Katherine often enjoys sleeping in late, as does Lord Brown. Miss Stewart, on the other hand, is usually one of the first to breakfast."

"Is that so?" Ezra felt suddenly more hopeful than he had all day.

"Just an observation." Lord Andrews picked up his fork, eying the plate of food that had just been placed before him.

Ezra picked up his own fork as well, but he didn't particularly care what was on his plate. His gaze flitted back to Grace, who was smiling brightly at Lord Brown, veritably hanging on his every word.

"Thank you," Ezra said at length.

Lord Andrews shrugged. "We all could use a little help from our fellow men at times such as these."

"Indeed." He probably needed more help than most, especially considering the letters he'd written—a mess of his own creation.

Waiting for the right opportunity to speak with her and further his own case clearly wasn't going to be enough. He would do as Lord Andrews had hinted and also be one of the first to breakfast in the morning. Perhaps then, he would be able to arrange some other time for them to be together. This may be Lord Brown's home, and the viscount certainly claimed far more charm than Ezra ever would, but Ezra wasn't about to throw his hands up in defeat.

Lord Brown led the men into the drawing room only five minutes after the ladies had left the dining room. The party's host immediately found his way to Grace and sat beside her on the settee. If that wasn't yet more evidence that he was forming designs on her, Grace wasn't sure what was. Unless, of course, one considered the way Lady Katherine looked daggers her direction when he did so. Grace knew she should feel no superior pride that Lord Brown was clearly seeking her out over the company of all others. And yet, wicked or no, she absolutely did. A tinge of self-assurance slipped through her, and she straightened her shoulders as she turned to Lord Brown.

"Did you enjoy the books you found in my library?" he asked her.

"Yes, I certainly did. It has been ever so long since I was able to read some new poems from Byron."

"He is rather bombastic, isn't he?"

Grace only stopped her scowl in time, smoothing it away before it could be noticed. "I would not say bombastic, exactly."

Lord Brown waved her comment away. "Regardless, I am happy you found something to your liking."

Lord Weston walked into the drawing room at that moment. Grace's gaze moved to him immediately, as did his to her. For a moment, she knew an intense desire to call him over to her. He of all people—she knew from their conversation earlier that morning—would stand by her in her defense of Byron. Did Lord Weston also love Shakespeare as much as she did? Grace very much wished to know.

And yet . . . she stopped herself. Yelling across the whole of the drawing room was surely uncouth. She didn't need to remind all the guests, Lord Brown especially, that she'd been raised without the fine polishing all the other ladies present had been blessed with.

Instead, she turned back to Lord Brown, wishing she was not so completely aware of Lord Weston moving to a very different place in the room.

"I did find some wonderful poems to entertain myself this afternoon. But what of you? What did you do for enjoyment?"

"Lord Andrews and his father, Lord Clark, joined me in the billiards room with Lord Honeyfield. We were trying to convince Lord Clark that a cue can strike the ball with far more accuracy than a mace. But as they say, it is hard for an old dog to learn new tricks."

"Have you a set of cues as well as a set of maces, then?" Grace asked. What her father would have given to have a billiards table at home.

"Indeed I do, and a fresh pair of new ivory balls to go with them."

"You should ask my father to play next time you would like a game."

"Does he enjoy the activity?"

"Most certainly. Only, he doesn't get to play as often as he wishes."

Someone moved up behind her; Grace felt certain she knew who it was as she'd not truly lost track of where in the room he stood since he'd walked in.

Lord Brown's gaze moved up and landed on the individual standing behind Grace. "And what of you, Lord Weston? Do you enjoy billiards as much as myself and Mr. Stewart?"

"I cannot claim to be a proficient." Lord Weston's deep voice rolled over her. "But I do enjoy the activity."

As the two gentlemen continued their talk about cues compared to maces, Grace momentarily closed her eyes and tried to compose herself. Why was it that Lord Weston never failed to upend her? Though, now that she thought on it, it wasn't an unpleasant sort of upending. There was nothing about him that put her on her guard or made her wish he would leave her be. His attentions were . . . constant. Kind. He agreed with her on several topics and seemed to share many of her same interests. Perhaps that was why he seemed to seek her out so frequently? She could think of no other reason. She was far too below him in station for either of them to ever consider being more than acquaintances; just the thought brought heat to her cheeks, and she had to duck her head to avoid drawing unwanted attention to herself.

"And what of you, Miss Stewart?" Lord Weston's deep voice brought her back into the conversation. "Do you prefer cues or maces?"

"Come now," Lord Brown said with a scoff. "A lady doesn't often play at billiards."

Grace turned toward Lord Brown, her eyebrow lifting slightly. Though he hadn't said the words aloud, his tone seemed to express that her opinion was inconsequential. "I played a few times with my father when visiting a neighborhood friend in my youth." She sat up straighter, turning toward Lord Weston once again. "I find I much prefer cues." Lord Brown could call her a bluestocking if he must, but in that moment, Grace felt no guilt in voicing a decided opinion. "I feel they shoot far straighter and give the player more control."

"I agree." Lord Weston's soft, sincere smile, which she'd only seen for the first time yesterday, reappeared. "Perhaps we might . . ." His gaze dropped as did his smile. Lord Weston shifted his weight, and yet he still did not finish his sentence.

"Are you asking a lady to a game of billiards?" Lord Brown said, disbelief in his tone as he glanced between Lord Weston and Grace.

Lord Weston looked toward the fire in the hearth, then back at her, his hand opening and closing a few times. "I . . . well . . ."

Lord Brown stood abruptly. "You'll never get the thing done that way. Let me show you how it's done." He offered his hand to Grace. "Would you accompany me to the billiards room, dear lady?"

Grace slipped her hand into his. "Sounds quite exciting."

Lord Brown helped her to her feet and tucked her hand beneath his elbow. "I would like for you to stand by me as my good luck charm while I show the Earl of Weston exactly how one wins with cues."

Oh . . . then she wouldn't be playing after all.

"I would be delighted," she managed to say while trying her best to hide her disappointment.

Lord Brown lifted his head. "Excuse me, may I have everyone's attention?"

The room stilled, and all eyes went to him. In the sudden attention, Lord Weston's smile completely vanished. There was a look about his eyes that Grace first believed was disinterest, perhaps even superiority. But the more she looked, the more it appeared to be discomfort she saw. Lord Weston did not appear to appreciate so many eyes on him.

She'd assumed he thought himself rather above all. But to look at him now, Grace couldn't help but wonder if she hadn't misjudged him.

"I declare," Lord Brown said loudly, "a competition between myself and Lord Weston, to be settled in the billiards room."

There were many *oohs* and some clapping at the announcement.

"More still," Lord Brown continued, "Miss Stewart has consented to be my lucky charm and will no doubt bring me much good luck."

"You're going to need it," Lord Clark called across the room.

Even more people laughed at that.

"What's the prize?" Lady Katherine asked.

Lord Brown placed a finger to his mouth, seeming to consider it. "Tomorrow, we will hunt for the perfect yuletide log and greenery to decorate the house. The winner will get help from three manservants in the endeavor, while the loser will have only his own eyes and the ones of those who take pity on him."

"All that, based on the outcome of a billiards game?" Lady Honeyfield asked.

"Why not?" Lord Brown said, turning to Lord Weston, his smile growing hard. "I like a good challenge."

The room stilled, and everyone seemed to be waiting to hear if Lord Weston would agree.

"Very well," he said at length. "Lead the way."

SIX

GRACE STOPPED FOR A moment, closed her eyes, and breathed in the winter morning air. The cold nipped at her cheeks and nose. She'd taken breakfast in her room that morning with her parents as Mother hadn't been feeling up to going downstairs after last night's long and late billiards game, which Father had insisted they all stay and watch.

But that hadn't stopped her from eagerly joining this morning's outing. She'd always loved hunting for evergreen boughs and her family's yuletide log.

"Miss Stewart," Lord Brown called from several paces away.

Grace opened her eyes once more. Nearly their entire group stood next to the viscount—everyone except a few of the older generation who'd stayed behind, and Lord Weston and the two who had chosen to accompany him, Lord Andrews and Lady Katherine.

"What do you think of this log?" Lord Brown said, pointing toward one stretching across the snowy ground beside him.

Grace lifted her skirts slightly and made her way his direction. Last night's billiards game had been enjoyable, she supposed. However, her mind had continually wandered to thoughts of just her and Lord Weston playing the game and how much more enjoyable that would have been. If only he had actually asked her instead of growing suddenly uncomfortable.

Then again, why an earl would ask a country girl of no great consequence to play at billiards with him, she couldn't imagine. Yet, he *had* rather appeared as though he was about to. If only Lord Brown had kept quiet a bit longer, perhaps Lord Weston would have.

Lord Brown still had his hand out, motioning toward the log before his feet. Grace mentally shook herself. Here she was doing it again, allowing her mind to wander to one man when *another* man was interested in her attentions here and now.

"I think it is a fine log," she said as her gaze dropped toward the fallen tree. "However, I worry it is too small. Bridgecross has such large hearths, I do not believe this one will burn all the way until Twelfth Night."

"I am confident it shall be just the thing. And remember, we must find a perfect log *before* the others." Lord Brown was taking this competition between himself and Lord Weston rather personally.

Grace pulled her lips to the side; she didn't feel confident in this selection at all. In previous years, she'd often ventured out with her father to hunt for the right yuletide log, and this one would hardly suit their small hearth at home. Squatting down, careful to keep her knees out of the snow so they wouldn't grow soaked, Grace rolled the log over and toward herself. The entire underside was gone, decayed until it was nothing more than a mushy pile of wet chips.

"I'm not even sure the servants could drag it back to the house without the thing completely falling to pieces," she said.

Lord Brown took hold of her elbow. With a gentle laugh, he pulled her back to her feet. "As a lady, you shouldn't dirty yourself so." He swiped at the bit of dirt on her gloves.

His nearness and touch were not lost on her. Granted, she didn't feel the heated awareness or rush of tingles that Byron often spoke of. She certainly felt no desire to take hold of Lord Brown and keep him near. Instead, she was almost overwhelmed with an urgent realization that he was proving his interest in her yet again. For the first time, the realization wasn't entirely welcome. That, mingled with a small dose of frustration that he'd been bothered by her willingness to get her hands dirty left Grace feeling unexpectedly uncertain.

Cupping both her hands in his, Lord Brown gave them a gentle pat. "If you truly dislike this log, we shall find another."

"Thank you, my lord," Grace said with a smile. Yet, she couldn't stop herself from pulling her hands out of his grasp.

Grace turned away from him even as Lord Brown called to the group that they would keep looking.

"Onward," he called. "We must find a better log than the others."

As the group continued forward, Grace slowed her step, allowing herself to fall behind. The interactions she'd just had with Lord Brown left her feeling unsettled. It wasn't that she disliked his attentions—she was here at Bridgecross Manor for the very purpose of encouraging him—only, she didn't like the way he'd held her hands as though she were a child in need of guidance and education. Though he'd acquiesced to her wishes to find a different log, his tone had sounded a bit condescending.

Grace shook her head, stopping her progress through the snow. This time, it wasn't to enjoy the lovely winter nip or the smell of fresh pine boughs. Grace folded her arms over her chest and looked about the forest. What was wrong with her? She was here *for* Lord Brown. Never in her wildest dreams had she ever considered catching the eye of a titled gentleman, let alone a viscount. Why, then, did she find herself so willing to put distance between them?

Her gaze landed on a form of black standing out against the forest of white and evergreen. Was that Lord Weston? He, Lord Andrews, and Lady Katherine had started off from Bridgecross Manor in a very different direction that morning. Then again, this was the densest part of the forest, so perhaps it wasn't so hard to believe both groups had found their way here. And what was he doing? He seemed to crouch low, but not in an effort to look over a log.

Was he hiding? The way he drew close to the ground, he appeared to be hoping to make himself smaller. And he huddled close to a group of several trees, peering out past their thick branches toward the direction he'd just come from.

Grace slowly made her way toward him. She'd found herself strangely disappointed when he'd lost at billiards the night before. It had been a close game the entire evening, Lord Brown scraping out the win at the last minute.

"Hello, Lord Weston," she whispered.

He whirled about, but when his eyes landed on her, his surprise gave way to relief. Standing fully, he brushed at his knees. "Hello, Miss Stewart." Though he didn't exactly whisper, he did keep his voice quite low.

"How does your hunt go?"

"Poorly, I'm afraid." Even as he answered, he glanced over his shoulder.

Grace looked about them as well. Though she could still hear Lord Brown and the rest of her group well off to the east, she couldn't see or hear anyone else. "Where are Lord Andrews and Lady Katherine?" she asked.

"Still searching, just off to the north a little way." He looked like he was trying to play it off as no unusual thing for such a small group to split up.

"And you thought you'd search this area of the woods on your own?" she pressed.

"Splitting up seemed a good idea."

A good idea to help him find the perfect log? Or a good idea to help him avoid certain people?

"Well," Grace continued, willing to let his solitude slide for now, "I feel I ought to warn you that Lord Brown is even more determined to win today's match between you two than he was at billiards last night."

"I must confess," Lord Weston said, resting a hand against the nearest tree. "I had no notion he was so competitive."

"No, nor I."

"Tell me, then, are you as eager to beat me as he is?" The smile that lit his face sent warmth straight to her heart.

"Generally, I am not." She couldn't help but smile in return. "Least ways, not competitive enough to avoid speaking with the enemy for a moment."

He placed a hand on his chest in feigned horror. "Oh, so I'm the enemy now? Is that it?"

Grace laughed softly. "Well, you *did* lose at billiards last night. And a refined lady such as myself could hardly be seen with someone who can't shoot a ball straight."

"I barely missed a single shot."

"It was still enough to lose, my lord."

He reached for her hand, unexpectedly taking it gently in his own. "You don't need to 'my lord' me." He gave her hand the softest squeeze. "Please."

Good heavens, if his gentle words and soft touch didn't send her heart into a furious gallop. What was he doing to her? Surely a gentleman so far above her own station did not usually show such familiarity. How, then, was she supposed to respond? Should she insist on continuing the formality their differences in station demanded?

Before she could manage a response, Lady Katherine's sharp tone reached them.

"I do not like Lord Weston going off on his own. I am sure we ought to find him."

Lord Weston took hold of Grace's arms and pulled her down, even as he dropped to his knees in the snow. The look on his face was utterly delightful. His eyes were wide and his jaw was tight, as though being found by Lady Katherine in that moment would be the most terrifying and horrifying thing ever. Grace bit down on her lower lip to stop the giggle that his expression, and the relief at not needing to respond, pulled from her.

He tossed her a sideways scowl, but one that was struggling against his own smile.

"I think he went more this direction," Lord Andrews replied.

"Come then," Lady Katherine said, "I am sure he will be most happy to see us again."

Their footsteps faded off, traveling further west.

Lord Weston let out a sigh of pure relief.

"I do believe you *are* hiding, my lord," Grace said, unable to stop her enjoyment at finding him thusly from slipping into her tone. Who would have guessed the forever-silent, serious-looking Lord Weston would be so fun to tease?

He pressed his lips into a straight line and gave her a flat stare. "Have you ever had to hunt for a yuletide log with her before?" He suddenly took hold of Grace's arm, clutching it to his chest. "Oh, Lord Weston." His voice was high-pitched and grating. "I just know you'll find us the perfect log for this Christmas. Oh, Lord Weston, you are so good at this. Oh, Lord Weston, how do you spot logs so well?"

Grace laughed, though she tried to keep it quiet, even as he gave a shudder and dropped her arm. She felt the cold against her at the loss of his touch immediately. More still, her fingers almost tingled with the wish to reach for him again. Which was odd. Thankfully, she managed to curb the strange impulse.

"You must forgive me," Lord Weston continued, returning to looking between the branches at the direction Lady Katherine and

Lord Andrews had taken. "I should not speak so ill of Lady Katherine."

Grace tucked her now cold arm up closer to herself. "She can be . . . persistent at times."

He gave a mirthless chuckle. "That's one way to say it."

"Then, you *are* hiding?"

Lord Weston's gaze dropped to the ground. When he lifted his head again, not only was there a small smile there, but he was also a bit red in the face. Grace could not remember ever seeing a man blush, let alone an earl. Yet she found it incredibly charming.

"Maybe?" he said at length, sounding as though he were asking a question.

Grace laughed again. "I am beginning to wonder if your punishment for loosing at billiards isn't, perhaps, rather too strict."

"I wouldn't have lost if it hadn't been for her." He took hold of her arm once more and ever so slowly helped them both to stand. Even as he spoke with her, his gaze was on the forest, no doubt watching for his teammates' dreaded return. "Lady Katherine, in her attempt to *support* me, stood rather too close and more than once bumped my cue."

Oh dear. Grace hadn't even noticed—probably because he hadn't said anything at the time. Lord Brown, on the other hand, had barked at a couple of people during the night for getting too close to him while he was trying to shoot. Lord Weston rose in her estimation, for he'd apparently dealt with the same thing and had chosen not to grow angry.

"You are a very patient man," Grace said, glad to be standing once more. Her legs had grown tired of crouching low.

"My sister gives me plenty of practice."

Grace swatted his shoulder. "I thought we already established you are not to speak ill of my dear friend."

The strangest look passed over Lord Weston's eyes at her statement. Or was it at her touch? She'd rather forgotten herself, she supposed. Just because he'd asked her not to 'my lord' him didn't mean she was on equal footing with him.

Instead of growing overbearing, his expression turned thoughtful. "May I ask you something?"

The jesting over, Grace clasped her hands before her. "Of course."

"Why did you continue to write my sister back?"

Her brow creased. "Why wouldn't I have?" Lady Frances had been a delightful correspondent.

"I mean . . ." Lord Weston paused. He placed a hand over his mouth, rubbing at his chin for a moment before starting again. "Was it in hopes of a connection with the sister of an earl? With someone who would elevate your own standing among society?"

It was a slap across the face. "Certainly not." Grace gathered her skirt in a fist. And here she'd started to believe Lord Weston didn't overly care for titles and place among the *ton*. "If you will excuse me, I believe I must return to my team."

Lord Weston skipped ahead, placing himself directly in her path. "I said that wrong."

She stopped but didn't respond.

"Forgive me. It is only that I have known many people to befriend . . . my sister . . . simply for such a reason." His voice lowered. "I was hoping to find you a better friend than that."

She supposed the sister of an earl *would* find it rather difficult to know who cared about her for herself and who wished only for the elevated connection. "I hate to think what Lady Frances has said to you to make you think so ill of me."

"Oh no, it was nothing in your letters. I only . . . wondered."

He seemed to sincerely wish to know. And did he know much of the content of her letters? Heat filled her cheeks. Lady Frances hadn't ever mentioned speaking of their letters to her brother. Truth was, she never mentioned him at all. Grace wouldn't have even known Lady Frances had a brother except she'd brought it up several times during their London Season. Lady Frances had seemed quite proud of having an earl for a brother, but perhaps that was simply part of the way she blended in among the *ton*. Her letters hadn't focused on such things at all.

In a large way, *that* was why Grace had continued the correspondence.

"I guess I found in your sister a soul quite similar to my own."

His smile returned. "I am pleased to hear it."

A cry of joy followed by a roll of laughter echoed among the trees. Grace turned toward the sound. It came from the direction Lord Brown had moved toward.

"It seems the perfect yuletide log has been found," she said. And yet, she felt no disappointment at not having been there for the find.

"Shall we go and see this glorious log for ourselves, then?"

Grace loved that he so quickly moved between that which was serious and that which was lighthearted; he was comfortable with either. At least he was when it was only the two of them. She was growing more and more certain that she was right in assuming Lord Weston did not feel himself superior to others. He was simply quiet and perhaps even a bit shy among large groups.

"I suppose we shall," Grace said, carefully making her way through the snow. "Although, once we do come upon the others, I'm afraid Lord Brown will make you confess to his superior log-finding abilities."

Lord Weston chuckled. "Ah yes, since such a skill is so highly sought after among society."

"Most highly sought after." A small root, hidden beneath the snow, caught on Grace's boot. She stumbled only a bit before righting herself. Her conversation with Lord Weston was far too diverting for her own good, apparently. "You shall have to confess to losing yet again. There is nothing else for it."

He took hold of her hand and gently wove it around his arm. The look he gave her sent warmth not only to her heart this time, but through all of her.

"Oh," he said, his gaze not leaving her. "I don't consider today a loss—not in the least."

SEVEN

"THAT IS A LOVELY tune, my dear," Mother said, walking over to stand beside Grace.

Had she been humming? Grace hadn't realized. Embarrassment skittered over her cheeks.

"I suppose I am looking forward to tonight's musicale," was all she could think to say. She kept her gaze on the mirror in front of her and on the reflection of her abigail, still busy pinning up her hair.

Mother glanced over at the maid's work. "That is quite lovely."

"Thank you, ma'am," the abigail said, giving a bit of a curtsy without dropping any of Grace's locks. Another couple of pins, and Grace was finished. She was feeling particularly pretty tonight, despite wearing a dress she'd worn many times and which had been altered more than once. Perhaps it wasn't so much that she was feeling pretty but that she was feeling excited about tonight's activity. Or she simply looked forward to whom she would get to speak, believing he wished to speak to her as well.

"Shall we go?" Grace stood, running a hand over the soft fabric of her skirt.

Mother stopped her with a hand on her arm. She waited quietly until the abigial had slipped from the room and they were alone.

"I wish to speak with you first, dearest."

Mother wasn't smiling. Grace slowly lowered herself back into the chair beside her dressing table.

Mrs. Stewart took hold of another chair, one seated by the window and perfect for reading, and drew it up closer to Grace. "I have rather noticed," Mother began slowly, "that you have taken a liking to spending time with Lord Weston."

Grace rolled her lips inward. She hadn't exactly thought overly about what others might think of their many conversations. They'd met at breakfast for the past many days, often talking and laughing for well over two hours. There had been several drawing room visits and a few strolls out into the snow together. It had all felt rather natural and easy. When she was with him, she often forgot anyone else was around. She shouldn't be so surprised that their time together hadn't gone unnoticed.

She could feel Mother waiting for a response. "He is a good man," she offered by way of explanation.

"So I have surmised."

She had? "So you think well of him?"

Mother's lips pursed. "That is not the point. The earl is a fine man, I grant you. But . . ."

Grace felt she knew where this was going. "But he's an earl."

Mother nodded. "Not only that, but his mother was the daughter of a marquess."

Grace hadn't known that.

"He is closely related to half of Parliament," Mother continued. "I have no doubt that he is quite pleasant to speak with, but please, do not lose sight of reality."

It was exactly the same argument Grace had made to herself countless times. Yet, hearing it aloud . . . it brought a biting pain, one that suddenly threatened tears.

"You mean," Grace said, "the reality that I am a nobody."

Mother cupped Grace's face in her hand. "You are not a nobody, Grace." Her gaze dropped momentarily, however, and when her eyes next met Grace's, they were sad. "Only, I believe it would behoove you to remember that Lord Brown invited us here. He is not nearly so elevated above us that society would balk at a connection between our families."

So Mother meant society *would* balk at a connection between herself and Lord Weston.

Of course they would. Hearing it from Mother shouldn't hurt so; Grace already knew as much.

She reached out and took Mother's hand. "You are right." She had been rather neglectful of Lord Brown. "I shall be more considerate tonight."

Mother gave her hand a squeeze and then rose. "Shall we go down, then?"

Grace nodded, but she wasn't so excited as she had been before. Walking beside Mother, they moved slowly through the corridor and down the stairs. All the while, Grace chastised herself. What had she been thinking, getting so wrapped up in her conversations with Lord Weston? Only a month ago, she'd been elated to receive Lord Brown's invitation here. Who gave up on a lifelong hope for security and comfort simply because a handsome, charming man had smiled at her?

A child did. That's who.

And that's exactly how Grace had been acting. Like a little girl, enamored with a strong jaw and a well-fitted jacket.

Lord Weston was a good, kind, engaging man. But he could not be her future.

And unless she wished for Lord Brown to give up on her, she'd better change her tune. She wasn't exactly a spinster, not yet, but there was no guarantee an offer as comfortable as Lord Brown's would ever come her way again. She was acting most unappreciatively in ignoring his attentions toward her.

As she and Mother reached the parlor, Grace dropped her shoulders and lifted her head. She sincerely hoped she and Lord Weston could still be friends.

But right now, she didn't need a friend.

She needed a future.

EIGHT

GRACE STEPPED INTO THE parlor, and hang him if Ezra didn't nearly drop the book in his hands. Gads, but she was stunning. The Pomona green dress she wore hugged her curves just right and accentuated her milky white skin. Her dark hair was piled atop her head with several curls falling about her face and along the curve of her neck. But what drew his attention the most was her pink lips and the way they tipped up in a smile.

He'd always imagined her smiling, all those months they'd written one another. The optimism in her letters, the way she chose to spend more time speaking of the good in her life than the bad, he'd known she must have an oft-used smile. He hadn't been wrong.

Ezra stood and strode toward her. She'd written him once of a dreadful musicale experience during the Season, one where her nerves had overcome her thoughts and Grace had felt certain the hostess was embarrassed afterward to admit to having asked her to play. He hoped she wasn't too nervous tonight. They were a smaller group, after all. Surely that would help. Either way, she ought to know he'd be cheering her on.

"Good evening, Mrs. Stewart, Miss Stewart." As he moved up beside her and her mother, Grace's eyes landed on him. Her smile grew, and her eyes sparked.

But then she cast her mother a sideways glance.

Her gaze dropped to the floor.

When next she looked up, it was not to smile at him but to offer him an indifferent nod of the head.

"Good evening, Lord Weston."

Her voice wasn't cold, but it certainly didn't contain the warmth and companionship he'd grown to expect from her. Perhaps she truly *was* nervous about tonight. But, no, that didn't seem quite right either.

"Are you feeling well?" he asked her, silently wishing her mother would go speak with one of the other matrons so he could truly and openly talk with Grace.

"My daughter is feeling quite fine," Mrs. Stewart answered. With that, she took hold of Grace's arm and led her around Ezra and further into the room.

Ezra stood, stunned, where they'd left him. He knew he often said the wrong thing while out among society; he wasn't charming or charismatic. But he was fairly certain he hadn't said anything wrong just now. All he'd done was wish them a good evening and ask after Grace's health. Perhaps he'd made it sound as though he believed she looked sickly? He wouldn't put it past himself to bungle even that small of an interaction.

Still, she *hadn't* looked all right. At least, not when she had looked at him.

Ezra ran a hand over the back of his neck. She'd smiled at him plenty that morning at breakfast. And what of Mrs. Stewart? He would bet his last shilling that she'd had something to do with the change in Grace.

The two women stopped directly before Lord Brown and struck up a conversation. Soon thereafter, Lady Brown stood up before the group and asked everyone to sit. They were ready to begin.

Ezra took the seat just behind and a little way down from Grace. He was too far away from her to strike up a conversation, but it was the closest seat still open and one blessedly close enough for him to overhear her conversation with Lord Brown.

Not that a true gentleman would ever eavesdrop; but a desperate, uncharming, slightly confused man certainly would.

"I am quite looking forward to hearing you play," Lord Brown said.

Ezra silently seconded the notion, while also cursing Lord Brown for being at liberty to say as much when he clearly was not.

"I would not have you get your hopes up," Grace responded. Her voice was soft and sweet as always, but he thought there was a tingle of impersonal formality to it as well. "I am no great performer."

"Modest to a fault, I'd say."

Ezra let out a huff. The way Lord Brown was forever dismissing Grace's words was growing incredibly frustrating.

"No." Grace's tone was a bit more insistent this time. "I am in earnest. While I love music, I'm afraid I have never been very good at the pianoforte."

"Then know that I am here," Lord Brown said, "cheering you on."

Curse Lord Brown. Those were supposed to be Ezra's words.

"In all honesty . . ." Grace's voice grew softer, and Ezra fought the urge to lean in to better hear. "I truly wish Lady Frances was here."

"Whatever for?"

"Because she is my dearest friend. If she were here in the audience, I know I would feel far less nervous now."

All the crawling restlessness, all the prickling frustration inside of Ezra melted at her words.

Lud, if only she knew. Her best friend *was* here, sitting in the audience now, silently wishing her all the best and knowing she would do magnificently at the same time.

But he couldn't tell her. Not here or now. He couldn't reach over, tap her on the shoulder, and give her a reassuring smile.

He couldn't buoy her up from the audience because she didn't know it was him.

It had only ever been him.

Several songs were performed, each slightly more challenging than the last. Lord Brown and Grace clapped politely at the end of each song, and they sometimes swapped polite commentary on the performances. All the while, Ezra's head was swimming. Grace needed her dearest friend right now, and thanks to his foolish missteps, she couldn't even have that.

Clapping sounded around him. Ezra followed suit, hitting his hands one against the other, but he couldn't even recall who'd played or how the song had sounded. Grace stood, and his gaze flew to her. Oh, how he wished he could stand up and tell her the truth. How he wished he could convey to her that her best friend *was* here. Her best friend believed in her and was sitting in the audience ready to offer encouragement.

Grace took a seat, positioned her hands above the keyboard, then glanced out over the crowd.

He willed her gaze to find his.

Finally, it did.

He gave her what he hoped was an encouraging smile.

I'm here, he wanted to say, *the friend you need now, to help you feel calm. It's me. I don't wear the face you expect, but I'm here, and I believe in you.*

Unfortunately, as Ezra was learning this Christmas, looks could only go so far. Grace's gaze left him, but her expression looked no less nervous than before. He'd failed her. As her dearest friend, he hadn't been able to be there for her in the way she needed—all because of a stupid misunderstanding.

She pushed a few keys and music floated out into the room.

Ezra's gaze stayed riveted on her. The song was simple. There were no overly elaborate arpeggios or long, drawn out trills. But it was lovely. A song made elegant in its simplicity. Though Grace may not have the quickest fingers or the fastest hands, she played with her heart, and the music took on a rare beauty because of it.

The song ended, and Grace slowly lifted her hands off the keys.

Ezra was on his feet immediately, clapping with enthusiasm. A movement out of the corner of his eye told him that Lord Brown, too, had risen to applaud her. This time, it didn't bother Ezra in the least that someone else was also acknowledging Grace. She deserved all the appreciation, in his estimation.

Indeed, Grace seemed a bit surprised to find not only an appreciative audience, but several individuals standing, as many had followed Ezra and Lord Brown's example. She turned a sweet pink, and her lips pulled up into a slightly embarrassed smile. Did she truly not have any idea how beautifully she had played? Then again, most often society mistook difficult and challenging for musical and elegant. Grace didn't, though, and it had shown in her music.

Grace gave a deep curtsy. When she stood, her gaze found his.

Ezra smiled at her, allowing all the pride he felt at hearing her play to shine through.

This time, it was clear she understood some of what he was thinking, for she smiled more brightly.

This time, it seemed, a simple look was actually enough.

NINE

"ARE YOU HEADING DOWNSTAIRS for breakfast?" Lady Augusta asked, crossing the corridor to stand beside Grace.

"I thought I might wait a bit before going down."

Lady Augusta's brow dropped. "You always go down first thing."

Grace hadn't realized her habits had been so noticed among the other guest at Bridgecross. Apparently, her lack of polishing school was making itself known again.

"True." Grace stumbled over the word. "But I thought I might enjoy some morning light through the window first." Actually, though she'd gotten up early same as every morning, it wasn't until she was dressed and in the corridor that she remembered her mother's admonition that she spend less time with Lord Weston and more with Lord Brown.

Now, she was stuck in the corridor, not wanting to return to her room, but knowing she shouldn't go to breakfast just yet.

"If you don't go, won't you be leaving a certain gentleman waiting for you?"

Grace's cheeks heated. Oh dear. She had been woefully wrong in assuming her time with Lord Weston was going unnoticed.

"I am sure he won't be put out," Grace muttered.

"Well, I'm not," Lady Augusta said.

Grace glanced up at the woman who had been a stranger only a few weeks ago but had easily become a comfortable friend. "I am from the country. My father holds no title. My mother has no lofty connections." Grace folded her arms tightly against her chest as she spoke, dropping her voice to be sure they weren't overheard. "Lord

Weston is an *earl*. Though we enjoy one another's company, I am not so deluded as to hope for anything coming of it."

Lady Augusta reached out and took hold of Grace's hand. "I understand what you're saying, and I hope you won't grow offended at what I wish to say in return." She waited, as though needing Grace's permission to continue.

Grace nodded. She wasn't sure she'd be happy with what her friend said, but she would hear her out, regardless.

"I know connections between two people from different stations is hard, and I wouldn't encourage you at all if I didn't feel very strongly about this. But do you remember when Lady Katherine mentioned the way Lord Weston supposedly looks at *all* women?" Lady Augusta dropped her voice. "All intense and brooding."

Grace smiled. How could she forget? It had been an extremely uncomfortable and humbling conversation.

"She was wrong," Lady Augusta continued. "Lord Weston doesn't look at *every* woman that way. He only ever looks that way when he's looking at *you*."

Grace's heart skipped a beat, then started again with a force so strong it seemed it might bruise her ribs. "Do you really think so?"

Lady Augusta gave her hand a squeeze.

"I would never encourage you in something I wasn't quite confident in. It's true I hesitated to say anything at all, only . . . I would hate it even more if assumptions led you to miss out on something magical this Christmas."

Grace didn't know what to say.

"He truly does look at you differently," Lady Augusta continued. "And the way he cheered for you last night? I would be hesitant to infer he only wants friendship."

Could Lady Augusta be right? Grace had never allowed herself to think of Lord Weston as anything more than a surprisingly considerate gentleman.

"I don't know what to do," Grace heard herself say.

Lady Augusta smiled, her gaze flitting up to the ceiling. "My dear friend Lady Lambert would say to be audacious. But what I think you need to do now is determine for yourself which man you prefer. Who is most likely to make you happy?"

What a strange thing to have happen to her, the simple Grace Stewart. The entire London Season had come and gone and not a single gentleman of her acquaintance had shown her the least bit of interest. Now, she had two men who were vying for her affection. At least, she did if Lady Augusta was to be believed.

"Now," Lady Augusta said, taking a step back. "I think I shall take breakfast in my chamber; leave the room downstairs open for others who wish for a more *private* conversation."

As Lady Augusta slipped into her room, a smile spread across Grace's face. Could her new friend be right?

And if she was, what then?

A thrill shot through her at the possibilities.

Clamping down on her smile, which was surely ridiculous at this point, Grace slowly made her way downstairs and into the breakfast room.

There Lord Weston stood, his back to her, a plate in one hand as he looked over the various foods placed out on the sideboard. Grace moved silently into the room.

He was a good head taller than her, and while not being particularly broad, he did fill his jacket nicely. He either heard her or sensed her, for Lord Weston glanced over his shoulder.

His gaze met hers, and he smiled. Good heavens, but he was a handsome man. Quite the paragon, in Grace's opinion, with his straight nose and firm jaw.

"I was beginning to wonder if I would be eating breakfast alone," he said.

When the entire party was gathered, Lord Weston's words often sounded aloof to the point of sometimes coming across as unfeeling. But when it was just the two of them, his voice was warm and inviting.

Grace reached for a plate at one end of the sideboard. "Judging by the amount of food already on your plate, you weren't exactly planning to wait for me on an empty stomach."

"Waiting is very strenuous work. A man has to fortify himself during times such as these."

Grace laughed. She still wasn't fully convinced, as Lady Augusta was, that Lord Weston would be willing to overlook her status in life and consider a more permanent connection between them.

Yet, when he laughed with her as he did now, she almost could.

"I suppose it's a good thing I came down when I did," Grace said, turning to the rich assortment of foods and adding some ham and boiled eggs to her plate. "I would hate to see what would have become of you if I had tarried."

Lord Weston broke off a piece of toast and popped it in his mouth, then grunted and nodded his head in agreement. "I would have withered away to nothing if not for my morning coffee." He turned and moved over to the table.

Grace didn't turn and ogle him as he walked away, though she was sorely tempted to. Instead, she picked up a mug.

"I prefer drinking chocolate myself." She ladled herself some, then joined him at the table, sitting directly beside him.

How easy it was to be with Lord Weston, laughing, teasing. And, heavens, that smile.

"I can't say that I've ever been one much for drinking chocolate," he said.

"Perhaps your cook wasn't preparing it well? The drink can be quite bitter."

"Is Bridgecross's cook any good?" He reached over and took hold of her mug.

At Grace's nod, he picked it up and took a long drink. It was strange, sitting beside him, talking, fully at ease as though this were merely another breakfast shared with a friend.

All the while, nothing felt the same. Was it only wishful thinking that made her see a spark in his eyes, a desire in his smile? Or had it been there before today, and she'd simply been blind to it? She wished she knew.

He pulled her mug away and studied it closely. "I think you may be right. If *this* is what drinking chocolate is supposed to taste like, then I understand why nearly every woman in England is so in love with it."

"There now, aren't you glad you waited for me to join you for breakfast? Otherwise, you'd still be ignorant."

He set her mug down, and this time, the smile he gave her was enough to melt the chocolate in her drink all by itself.

"Oh, Miss Stewart," he said, his voice suddenly low and warm. "You are always worth the wait."

Her breath caught in her throat. Dear angels above.

His lips ticked upward in a half smile, and Grace found she would have been quite content looking into those robin-egg blue eyes all day. He looked so sincere. And his tone was so forthright.

Could he truly be developing feelings for her?

In that moment, she felt quite certain she was developing feelings for him. Feelings she'd been too scared to admit to before. But now? It was looking more and more likely that Lady Augusta had been right.

Voices echoed about the corridor just outside, and they both shifted, returning their gazes to their plates. Lord Clark entered the room, leaning heavily on his walking stick and followed closely by his son, Lord Andrews.

Grace picked up her fork and tried to stab a bit of ham.

Next to her, she felt Lord Weston stiffen a bit. He always did whenever the room grew very crowded. How blessed she felt that he was willing to relax and show his true self to her.

Lord Brown and his mother entered the room next. And if the sounds that continued to bounce around the corridor outside were any indication, the rest of the party would be breaking their fast soon enough.

Lord Brown's gaze found hers. Grace held it a bit longer than usual. It seemed to her that Lady Augusta had been right on another score—she did owe it to herself and to both these gentlemen to determine whom she preferred.

It was time she did just that.

TEN

"AND WHAT DO YOU think of the view, Miss Stewart?" Lord Brown asked as he patted her hand where it rested against his arm.

Grace tore her attention away from his touch—and how little it did to her heart—and tried to focus on the gently falling snow across the back lawn.

"It is a very lovely view," she said, her tone far from enthusiastic.

"I believe any woman of refinement would find this view most enjoyable all year around."

"I suppose so." Grace still could not drum up the excitement Lord Brown seemed to think such a vista should inspire. Ah well, she knew the reason. It was because the *man* beside her had ceased to elicit anything in her. While Lord Brown continued to look out the large window in the drawing room, pointing out a few particular points of interest, Grace allowed her gaze to land on him.

How was it that only a few weeks ago, the mere mention of Lord Brown had brought her such joy, and now it led her to feel absolutely nothing?

When had the change begun? She couldn't say. Her infatuation with the baron was over before she'd even realized it was waning. How odd it now felt to stand beside him, the very man who'd inspired many a dream in her not so long ago, and feel indifference.

Not that he wasn't a good man. Not that any woman wouldn't be blessed to have a connection with him.

Only, she found she was not longing for that connection herself.

Good heavens, what was she going to tell Mother?

She'd never understand.

"Miss Stewart," came a deep familiar voice. Lord Weston's voice.

His, however, was like a yule log blaze, one that warmed her completely through. Grace turned, letting Lord Brown's arm drop away, and curtsied to Lord Weston and Lady Katherine.

"Good afternoon to you both," she said, though she barely could force her gaze away from Lord Weston.

His smile was small—no broad grin that spread ear to ear—yet it seemed sincere, and Grace even believed she saw a spark of something more. A promise? A desire?

Her heart lurched at the notion. Grace turned her head away so he wouldn't see her blush. How could such a mundane, unremarkable expression as a simple smile elicit such intense heat inside her?

"Lord Weston had a marvelous idea just now," Lady Katherine said, addressing them all but not bothering to ever look directly at Grace. "He proposed we all take a sleigh ride. Last night's snowfall undoubtedly rendered the nearby forest quite magical." She squeezed Lord Weston's arm.

A strange surge of biting discomfort swelled in Grace.

Jealousy, Grace was quickly learning, was not a pleasant emotion.

Lady Katherine reached for Lord Brown with her spare hand, looping it around his arm and pulling him to her so that she had a man standing on either side. Grace didn't miss the small look of triumph Lady Katherine shot her. "Won't it be glorious all riding together?"

"It is a good idea," Lord Brown said, "however, won't Lady Augusta, Lord Andrews, and Mr. Banfield care to join us? Not to mention my mother. She's never been one to turn down a sleigh ride. We'll have to split up and take three sleighs, at least."

"Do you have so many?" Lady Katherine asked him, her tone taking on a fake quality, as though astonished at the prospect.

Lord Weston's gaze slid to Grace and his look clearly said he saw straight through Lady Katherine's ruse. They shared a smile.

Lord Brown, for his part, only puffed his chest out. "I do indeed have many fine vehicles. I shall have them readied at once, and just as soon as you ladies are dressed in your warmest, we shall be off."

"I cannot wait," Lady Katherine said with a giggle. "It will be such fun to see the lovely countryside beside two handsome men."

Seeing the three of them together rather irked Grace. She'd known many women like Lady Katherine during her Season. Ladies who needed all the attention, all the men, all the compliments and praise. Grace was tired of it. Of the games and posturing. She wanted to spend some time with her friend, the man who filled her mind while also heating her heart. Rather than making her feel less important, as Lady Katherine was no doubt trying to do, all her silly antics left Grace feeling rather bold.

"Yes," Grace said, "I'm afraid I *have* been monopolizing all of Lord Brown's time this morning. Of course you would want to ride with him." Grace slid her hand around Lord Weston's arm. "Shall we go tell the others of your idea?"

Without allowing anyone a moment to respond, they walked out of the room, leaving a silent Lord Brown and a stunned Lady Katherine behind.

"That was smoothly done," Lord Weston said, his voice low.

"I wanted to spend some time with my friend," she said, choosing to leave out her other reasons. Like how she was finding it harder and harder to deny the strong pull she felt toward him. Like how her hope was growing to the point where it might crush her. Like how she was beginning to feel nearly desperate to know if he would ever see her as more than just a friend.

Lord Brown proved correct in assuming that the other young people would care to join them, as would his mother. When they heard that Lady Brown would be going out, Lord and Lady Honeyfield chose to also join. In the end, they were to make a nice even company of five couples. With that all set, everyone hurried to their rooms to ready themselves. Grace changed as quickly as she could, donning her warmest everything—warmest under clothing, warmest dress, warmest pelisse—as well as a thick muff and bonnet trimmed with fur.

When she stepped out of doors, three elegant sleighs were lined up before her. The horses stamped impatiently, two, then three of them tossing their heads. Grace exhaled at the beauty of the snow-dusted trees around her, and her breath came out as a small cloud, billowing about her cheeks.

Winter truly was a beautiful time of year.

Lord Weston stepped up beside her, his hand going to the small of her back. His touch was like brushing up against a warming block. Perhaps she ought not have troubled herself with dressing quite so warmly. If Lord Weston continued to affect her so, she wouldn't need the extra layers.

"The first two sleighs," he said, his low voice only making her heart race more, "each carry four individuals. But I thought we should claim the last sleigh before anyone else does."

The last of the three sleighs was smaller, appearing only big enough for two and a driver.

"If you wouldn't mind?" Lord Weston asked, his tone sounding a touch less confident.

Grace couldn't help but smile. "I think that last sleigh is lovely." And not only because it would guarantee some time for just the two of them. The small sleigh was decked out with straps of silver bells, and draped atop the bench seat was a warm-looking, vibrant red blanket.

Lord Weston led her over to the open-top sleigh and held the door as she climbed in. Grace picked up the blanket as she sat and found a heated brick already down by her feet. Lord Weston settled beside her, and Grace fluffed the blanket out and over their laps. There was something intensely intimate about sharing a blanket. Though they sat close, they weren't touching. And yet, the blanket seemed a sort of connection all the same, a link that drew them in toward one another regardless of the space between them.

Soon, the rest of the party had gathered and were settled in the first two sleighs. If anyone was annoyed or pleased that Grace and Lord Weston had commandeered the last, small sleigh for themselves, Grace couldn't tell. She was having too hard a time focusing on anything other than the man beside her and how desperately she wished she could remove her pelisse without looking like an addlepated fool.

With a few calls to the horses, first one then the second sleigh started off. Hers and Lord Weston's sleigh started with a small jump, pushing them both back in their seat and somehow managing to drive them closer to one another. Though that could have been Grace's imagination. Or perhaps she wasn't the only one feeling the pull?

Good heavens, she was going to burn up beneath this blanket. Yet she didn't want to pull it off either.

Lord Weston said something, but the sound of the jingling bells drowned out his words.

"What was that?" Grace asked.

Lord Weston leaned in close, his mouth just above her ear. "I said its beautiful, isn't it?" His warm breath was not helping her avoid overheating.

Still, she leaned in toward him all the same. There were, after all, worse ways to die. "Absolutely breathtaking."

They rode for a minute or two in silence, both drinking in the white elegance around them. More still, drinking in the feel of being together. At least, Grace hoped she wasn't the only one doing as much. If Lord Weston had been a man nearer her own station, she would certainly believe he fancied her. She could no longer deny that he sought her out, that he was relaxed and at ease around her in a way he wasn't with others. She'd thought herself conceited when she first comprehended such a thing, but she'd experienced too many interactions which validated the idea for her to question it now.

And yet . . . he was an earl and she the daughter of a gentleman of no title. That he would ever take notice of her was most unexpected. He certainly hadn't earlier that year, during the London Season. But she had learned over these several weeks that he wasn't comfortable among society. It was possible that her connection to his sister made Lord Weston feel, when he first arrived at Bridgecross Manor, as though he could relax a bit around her. It was rather a blessed surprise that they found in one another someone whose company they enjoyed so immensely.

"It's a shame Frances isn't here with us now," Grace said. "I know she is partial to riding through the snow."

Lord Weston tensed beside her.

Odd, that. They hadn't spoken often of Lady Frances, but the few times they had, she'd gotten the impression brother and sister were on well enough terms.

"Actually," Lord Weston said, drawing the single word out longer than usual. He shifted about until his hand rested atop her forearm, a few of his fingers finding their way inside her muff. It wasn't exactly a scandalous touch, but her heart reacted as though it were. "I want to speak to you about Frances."

Grace turned slightly, angling toward him so that it was easier to hear his words. Though it was for purely practical purposes, she didn't miss that it was perfectly easy to slide in and rest against his shoulder, that she and Lord Weston fit together most deliciously.

"Earlier today," he began, "you called us friends. Did you mean it?"

ELEVEN

EZRA WAITED.

And waited.

She was going to respond, wasn't she? Surely she at least considered him a friend.

His fingertips, warm beneath her muff, itched to stretch out and find Grace's hand. To entwine his fingers with hers. To hold her hand against his own. Perhaps pull her hand to his mouth and kiss each of her fingertips.

"Do you consider me a friend?" Grace asked at length.

"Of a surety." How could she even ask? Though she was—which meant he must be mucking things up between them something awful.

Grace didn't move from where she sat so near him—a fact he found completely diverting—but her brow fell, and her lips pulled to one side.

"Even all things considering?" she asked.

A sticky, prickly fear worked its way up his back. "Considering what?" Did she know? How could she have found out?

Grace looked away, her fur-lined bonnet blocking his view of her expression. His back went stiff. Though, perhaps this was for the best. This was what he wanted, after all, for her to know it had been him writing her this entire time.

Grace's voice was soft. "You will not think ill of me if I speak plainly?"

That could either be a good thing, or a very, very bad thing. "I wish you would."

She turned to face him. Her gaze was intense, as though she were reading him. It wouldn't surprise him if she could understand all he was thinking and feeling by simply looking in his eyes. After all, she'd read so many of his words, so many of his thoughts and beliefs, it only stood to reason she would also be able to read his face.

"I am sure," she began, her words slow and deliberate, "you are not unaware that my father holds no title."

What?

Ezra stared at her.

What the blazes did that have to do with anything?

He couldn't find words, he was so dumbfounded.

Her eyes dropped away from him. "I realize there is a large chasm between your station and mine. Though I have enjoyed our time together, I would never dream—"

Ezra reached for her chin, cupping it softly and bringing her gaze back to him. Her eyes were wide and unsure.

"Do you honestly believe such a thing would matter to me?" But how could she not wonder? She didn't know the very individual she'd come to know all these months through their letters was him.

She was right. There was a chasm between them. But not one of station, status, or situation. It was that *he* knew her so well, of her dreams and hopes and thoughts. She knew such things of him too, only she didn't know it *was* him. Instead of bridging the chasm all these weeks by spending time together, in that moment, it felt as though Ezra had only made the separation more pronounced.

His thumb, almost of its own accord, slowly stroked her cheek. "I do not care what your family's current situation is." It was a pitiful beginning. He needed to keep going. Needed to tell her everything.

That it had been him all along. That he was the one who knew her so well, that he was the one she knew so well.

He needed to explain how it had all begun, that he'd only ever meant to send a bit of encouragement to a young woman he knew to struggle with large crowds, much as he did. He'd never intended to deceive her, for this thing between them to grow to consume his entire life.

And yet it had. She was all he'd ever wanted. She was the only one he cared to love.

Except, instead of speaking anything at all, his gaze dropped to her lips. They stood out pink against her milky skin. She breathed out in time with him. A cloud formed between them in the winter air, momentarily obscuring his sight of her. Yet, her eyes continued to stand out through the fog they'd created, piercing him straight to the heart.

He tipped her chin up, bringing his head closer to hers. She settled in, leaning against him in kind.

A man could wish for nothing more than to look into such eyes and hold such a woman every day.

His lips brushed lightly over hers. Not a kiss, merely a light touch. A question. A hope.

The sleigh rocked to a sudden stop. Grace's hand shot out of her muff, and she steadied herself with a hand on his chest. They were back at the house. Up ahead, the rest of the party were quickly climbing out of the other two sleighs, chatting and laughing gaily. Grace quickly withdrew her hand, slipping it back into her muff.

Lord Brown was quickly striding their direction. Ezra cleared his throat and sat up straight. A sliver of frigid air slipped down between himself and Grace. Space was necessary, but certainly far from welcomed.

"How was your ride, Miss Stewart?" Lord Brown asked, opening the door and offering her his hand.

She slipped her hand into his and Ezra forced himself to look away. He needed a moment to collect himself before he faced the others again.

"It was quite lovely," Grace said, her voice sounding slightly winded.

Ezra's stomach flipped. Was she merely saying that for Lord Brown's benefit? Or had she truly considered their time together lovely? No, not just lovely, *quite* lovely. He didn't dare look up for fear he'd catch her eye and he wouldn't be able to maintain the needed air of unaffectedness. Because if there was one truth he'd thoroughly learned, it was that nothing about Grace left him unaffected.

The sleigh bounced slightly as Grace stepped down. Ezra fought against the urge to bury his face in his hands. Grace and Lord Brown moved further away. Would she look back at him? Give him any indication that she would have welcomed the touch? It was better if he didn't know. One look from her and he might scandalize every guest here by leaping from the sleigh, wrapping her in his arms, and kissing her soundly.

Gads, what a disaster that would prove.

Instead, he kept his head turned away and his hands firmly planted in his lap. Their voices moved further and further away, and Ezra felt every inch of distance between himself and Grace.

He'd nearly kissed her. He'd all but done so. What had he been thinking? He was already risking everything by keeping the truth from her for this long. He'd only been waiting until she could handle the idea of being a dear friend with Lord Weston, not just Lady Frances, before admitting the truth. Not that he had a clear answer on that accord now.

She hadn't exactly answered his question.

Then again, neither had she run or pushed him away when he . . .

The thought of what had almost happened continued to warm him, radiating from his chest outward.

Yet, he could not do so again. Not until Grace knew the truth. Ezra pushed himself to his feet, taking in the sight of the other sleighs, now both empty, and the last few members of the house party not yet to walk inside. Ezra stepped down, his boots crunching through the snow. He needed to be more careful. He couldn't risk losing Grace, not at this point. He would have to find an excuse to speak with her alone. That wasn't bound to be easy. But it needed to happen. The sooner the better.

After that, if she cast him aside, he would have to face as much. Perhaps he'd follow her back home after the house party ended and endeavor to court her there. He'd write her letter after letter if necessary. Frances would be most put out by him, but he didn't care. The sounds of sleighs moving through the snow and toward the carriage house echoed behind him. If Ezra's hopes were to come true, then Frances would soon be sisters to the very woman she believed herself too high to even correspond with not many months ago. Ezra laughed softly to himself. Oh, the irony.

"Ezra!"

He froze at the call, which had come from behind him. That sounded most markedly like . . .

But it couldn't be. Surely she wouldn't have come. Ezra was only imagining things since he'd been only now thinking of his sister.

"Ezra!" A woman ran over to him, catching hold of his arm and smiling up at him from beneath her expensive hooded cape, dressed in the finest of traveling gowns. "Surprise!"

Ezra didn't have words to say.

Instead, he stared down at the last person on earth he wished to see. Lady Frances.

TWELVE

GRACE NODDED POLITELY AS Lord Brown spoke on and on regarding . . . something. She wasn't even fully sure what their conversation was composed of anymore. She only knew that her hand still rested around his arm and that Lady Katherine had claimed his other arm and was speaking most animatedly with him.

Seeing them like this, each trying to outshine the other as they walked into the parlor, it was quite clear how perfect they were for one another. They both craved society and attention and being seen as fashionable. More still, Grace was growing more and more certain that, while his intentions may have been different at the start of the house party, at this point, Lord Brown pursued her mostly in an effort to out-game Lord Weston. Likewise, Lady Katherine seemed to be sinking her claws further into Lord Brown only because she wished to out-maneuver Grace.

What a mess they both were—and so well suited. Could they not see that themselves? A few weeks ago, Lord Brown had wished for Grace, and Lady Katherine had believed herself wanting Lord Weston, but perhaps Lord Brown and Lady Katherine would find the matches they'd been hoping for this holiday after all.

Grace was more than happy to relinquish any supposed hold on Lord Brown that Lady Katherine clearly believed she still had. He was all hers. As they continued on and on, Grace stayed silent, allowing her mind to wander back to what had just happened.

She was more than happy to keep to herself as she relived what had been and pondered what almost was.

For days now, she'd been hoping Lord Weston might be willing to see past her station and just see her. His words still rung inside her mind. *Do you honestly believe such a thing would matter to me?* She smiled at the memory.

The door opened and a footman stepped in. "Lady Frances Stanhope, my lord."

Lady Frances had come? Grace turned quickly to the door. She'd not expected her friend to join them this holiday. What a joyous surprise.

Lord Weston stepped into the room first. His gaze caught hers. His brow was creased and the look he gave her—gracious but his expression was hard to read.

Lord Brown led her and Lady Katherine over. "Lady Frances, we had not expected you."

"But I hope my surprise arrival is not unwelcome," Lady Frances said with a flutter of her lashes.

"Certainly not," Lord Brown continued. "I trust you already know Miss Stewart and Lady Katherine."

Grace could not stay quiet any longer. "Lady Frances and I are very good friends." She turned to the woman. "I am so happy you have come in time to join us for the Twelfth Night ball."

"Yes," Lady Frances said, her gaze sliding over to Grace and traveling down the full length of her dress.

Grace was quite suddenly put in mind how worn out her dress was, how it was decidedly last year's fashion. There was just something about the way Lady Frances looked her over that made her smile slip.

"Frances, *my* dearest friend," Lady Katherine said, stepping forward and pressing her cheek up against either of Frances's. "I am so glad you were able to make it." She turned and faced Lord Brown. "I hope you will also forgive my meddling. When I saw our numbers were so uneven, I wrote to this lovely creature and asked her to join us."

Lady Katherine and Lady Frances stood shoulder to shoulder, arms intertwined, and faced Grace.

It was as though they'd become a wall, one standing between her and whatever they wished her *not* to obtain.

Grace could understand this type of petty action from Lady Katherine, but Lady Frances? Where was the woman who had agreed with her that autumn was magical and that lemonade should always be made extra sweet? Where was the friend who had written her words of comfort and cheer?

"I long for a game of whist," Lady Katherine said suddenly. "Don't you?"

"Quite so," Lady Frances agreed immediately. "Lord Brown, would you join us? You and Lady Katherine can sit opposite myself and my brother."

Grace felt the women's dismissal like a slap across the face. This was not at all the woman she'd come to believe was her friend. Had something happened between their last shared letters and now?

"Frances," Lord Weston grumbled low, "you will remember your manners."

Lady Frances only turned her nose up at him. "I would be happy to have Miss Stewart join us. Only, Lady Augusta is endeavoring to keep both Lord Andrews and Mr. Banfield entertained on her own." Her smile grew taut. "Surely one as kind and considerate as Miss Stewart would far prefer helping another than seeing to her own amusement."

"Then," Lord Weston said, throwing Grace an apologetic glance, "we shall simply have to ask the three of them to join us as well."

The evening did not prove enjoyable to Grace. Every time a new game was mentioned or a new activity set upon, Lady Kathrine and Lady Frances connived to squeeze Grace out. The two women all but glued themselves to Lord Brown and Lord Weston's sides. By the time dinner was announced, Grace was ready to cry off for the entire evening and see herself to her bedchamber.

What had happened that had caused her friend to turn on her so absolutely?

As the rest of the party began filing out of the parlor and toward the dining room, Grace silently made her way over to Lady Brown.

"I beg your pardon, my lady," she began, her voice soft. "But I fear I have a terrible headache coming on. I think it would be best if I took dinner in my own room tonight."

"Oh, what a shame," Lady Brown said, giving Grace's arm a gentle pat.

"You can't slip out before dinner." Somehow, Lady Katherine had managed to spot Grace and intercept her. "We are only now finally an even number. If you were to miss dinner tonight, we will be uneven still."

Grace didn't turn to look at the woman. Instead, she chose to close her eyes momentarily and take a deep breath.

"I find it terribly inconsiderate," Lady Frances's voice reached Grace next, "for a lady to *cry off* when doing so would clearly make everyone else uncomfortable."

"Indeed, quite inconsiderate," Lady Katherine agreed.

Grace was too tired and far too confused to deal with this right now. She could not fathom how Lady Frances had gone from the light-hearted, supportive friend of her letters to this petty and manipulative woman before her now in only a few weeks' time. It made no sense.

"Come now, ladies," Lady Brown said, her voice clearly trying to placate. "If Miss Stewart says she is unsuited to dining with us tonight, we ought to extend her some grace. No doubt she shall join us again tomorrow." Lady Brown turned toward Grace. "I will instruct a maid to bring you a tray in your room."

"Thank you, my lady." Grace curtsied, but then left without so much as a parting word to either Lady Katherine or Lady Frances.

The house was dark, the winter sun having set over an hour ago. Candles in sconces lined the stairway but cast off only small puddles of yellow light, none stretching far enough to blend into the next. Grace moved from one bubble of light to the next, careful not to trip on her way up. The house was colder in the passageways and corridors as well. She would do well to remember a shawl next time she left her room.

And yet, it wasn't only the temperature of the air that sent a chill through her.

The confusion of the day rested against her, weighing her down. Grace was no longer agitated by uncertainty; she'd been clearly pushed out of the way and shoved aside enough today to feel only cold bewilderment. The corridor which led to all the guest bedchambers stretched out before Grace. At the end was a tall, narrow window. She passed her own door and moved toward it.

White snowflakes slowly drifted down, covering up the tracks made earlier by the sleighs.

Her mind flitted back to the moments before Lady Frances's arrival. Back to when she'd sat beside Lord Weston. Back to when he'd almost kissed her.

How filled with elation she'd been in that moment.

How horribly different she felt now.

"Grace." Lord Weston's deep voice sounded behind her.

She spun to find him standing only a few steps away, hands clasped behind his back. She couldn't make out of much his expression, but he seemed apprehensive. Much as he had looked when he'd first entered the parlor with Lady Frances at his side.

Grace lifted her chin. Far from being pleased to see him, she was angry.

Inwardly, she knew his sister's actions were not his fault, and he had tried to stand up for her repeatedly throughout the day. But it had only seemed to urge Lady Frances and Lady Katherine on. How could he make her feel so wanted one minute, and then not even tell her that his sister was coming? How could he not tell her that his sister had never meant any of the nice things she'd said in her letters? How could he have not warned her of Lady Frances's vitriol?

"I have not given you permission to use my Christian name, my lord." Grace's words came out tight.

He ran a hand down his face. "No. Forgive me."

They stood before the window, cold air wafting down over them.

"I need to explain," Lord Weston said at length.

Then something *had* happened. "I have been wondering what would have changed Lady Frances's opinion of me so decidedly."

He tipped his head, first one direction then the other. "It is rather more complicated than that."

Tears pricked Grace's eyes. "Were all her letters nothing but lies, then? A game, in her mind?" A plan to lead on the poor young woman from the country, the one with no claim to status or wealth. Is that all this was?

"It is true," he said softly, "that my sister places far too much importance on titles and standing among society."

Grace turned away from him, humiliation burning against her face. "If she didn't care to associate with me, she didn't have to write back." Her words dropped as she muttered to herself. "No one else did."

Lord Weston took two steps closer to her. Even in the dark, she could see the swirls in the silk of his waistcoat and the muted glint of moonlight on his buttons.

"What do you mean, no one else did?" he asked.

Grace drew herself up but still struggled to fight off the humiliation clinging to her. Lord Weston clearly knew of his sister's misuse of her, he might as well know the whole of it. "I first wrote your sister in July of this year. My family had to leave London early, and I was feeling rather sorry for myself for not being able to enjoy the entire Season in Town. During a particularly lonely morning, I sat down and wrote nearly two dozen letters, all to various acquaintances I'd met earlier that year." As lonely as she'd been that morning, writing letter after letter, it was nothing compared to the utter rejection she'd felt for the next several weeks, waiting for replies that never came.

"Your sister," Grace said, "was the only one who ever responded."

"London is full of idiots."

Grace couldn't stop the guffaw that escaped her. It wasn't a London full of idiots that hurt her, it was a London full of prim ladies all too good to associate with the likes of her.

"I wish she'd never written me back at all," Grace continued, folding her arms against the cold.

"Don't say that."

"I am in earnest." She stared at Lord Weston. "If her only aim was to laugh silently behind my back, to use me for her own enjoyment, then she ought never to have written—"

"She didn't write you back."

Grace stared at Lord Weston, not fully understanding what he'd just said. She understood the words clearly enough, but she couldn't wrap her mind around his point in saying them.

He placed a shoulder against the wall beside the window and leaned heavily against it. "Frances never wrote you back. I did."

The floor seemed to tip beneath Grace's feet. *He'd* written her back? What did that even mean? What was he saying?

"Then . . ." Grace took a small step backward. "*You* have been laughing at me this whole time as well?"

"No." The word burst from him, firm and resolute. He reached out, taking both her arms in his hands. "Please let me explain."

Her head was spinning. She wished to pull away from him, but she wasn't fully sure she could stand just now without his hands holding her up. So she stood still and waited.

Lord Weston must have taken her silence as permission to continue. "When your letter arrived, Frances and I were both in the room. It was clear, by the way she acted, that Frances had no desire to further an acquaintance with you. I felt she was being overly prudish and, in an effort to make her see how childish she was acting, I read your letter aloud to her."

"You had no right," Grace heard herself say. Though it hardly sounded like her own voice.

"You are correct, but I wanted Frances to see that ignoring someone simply because their father held no title was wrong."

Grace shivered. "But I did receive a letter."

Lord Weston shrugged off his jacket. "In reading your letter, I saw a woman who felt much as I did." He draped the jacket over her shoulders, pulling it snug against her. "I have often struggled among society. You were so honest in your expression, I found I couldn't allow it to go unanswered, no matter my sister's smallness of character."

His jacket was warm from his body heat. It smelled of him too. Strange that she should know it to be *his* smell. She hadn't consciously labeled Lord Weston's scent before. But smelling it now, she recognized it all the same.

"I wrote you," he said. "I wrote you and signed my sister's name to protect you from scandal."

It was true. If he'd written her and signed his own name and word had gotten out, she would have been ruined. Grace pulled his jacket closer around her still, subtly lifting one of the lapels closer to her cheek. "So all this time?"

"It's been me."

Those three simple words brought everything she'd believed for months to a sudden end. She and Lady Frances were not friends, never had been.

"It's always been me," Lord Weston said, his voice softer than before.

Her mind threw up letter after letter, confession after confession, for her to remember. Grace folded her arms, her brow creasing. She'd shared more than just the comings and goings of her life. She'd shared private thoughts and hopes. Good heavens—she pressed a hand over her eyes—she'd written to him regarding her first fluttering feelings regarding Lord Brown. How flattered she'd been he'd invited her. How much she'd hoped it meant he intended to further their connection.

She wasn't humiliated now for the same reasons she'd been before —now at least she knew no one had been secretly laughing at her behind her back—but she felt humiliated all the same. She'd thought she'd been writing to another *woman*. She never would have worded her letters in such a way had she known she was writing a gentleman.

What must he think of her?

Grace spread her fingers and peered between them. In the dark corridor, he waited, silently watching her. He didn't move or speak, and neither did she.

The longer she stood there watching him watch her, the more she realized how much she *didn't* know what he was thinking. She didn't know what he thought of her or what this meant. Her hand fell away from her face. So many words hung unspoken between them. But she didn't know what they were. She didn't know how he felt about her. She wasn't even sure she knew how she felt about *him*. Not now. Not after all this. Earlier today, things had seemed so clear, but now, everything was a mess. A tangled web of duplicity and half-truths and who knew what else.

Grace dropped her arms to her sides, allowing the jacket to slide down and off her. The cold bit against the bare skin of her arms between her sleeves and gloves.

She held out the jacket. "I think I shall retire to my bedchamber now."

Lord Weston took the jacket but held it limp in his hand and made no move to put it back on. "Please, you must see that I never intended to hurt you."

"Must I?" she said. "Honestly, I don't know what I believe." She was too tired, too worn down from all the intense emotions of the day to know up from down. "Good night, Lord Weston."

She didn't give him time to respond but walked quickly to her room and shut the door firmly behind her.

THIRTEEN

BREAKFAST THE NEXT MORNING was a quiet affair as only Lord Weston was present, with his plate of eggs, toast, and ham. Grace had come down every morning for weeks. The room felt far too large and echoed far too much without her. He picked at his eggs with his fork. He didn't blame her for not coming down. The lie he'd been perpetrating was no small one.

Voices from the corridor outside told him he wouldn't be alone for long.

The door open and Lord Brown walked inside, Grace on his arm.

Ezra's stomach turned a sharp flip. Grace greeted him with a smile, but it was a fake one. He knew her too well now. The spark in her eyes which he'd come to love was missing. The sincere optimism was lacking. And it was all his fault.

Grace and Lord Brown made their way to the sideboard and began filling their plates. They talked easily of the day promising fine weather and of their thoughts on that evening's Twelfth Night ball. Grace stayed close to Lord Brown, making it painfully clear she had no desire to speak with Ezra. Soon, the others entered the room. Lord Andrews gave him a sympathetic smile. Apparently the fact that he and Grace had had a falling out was not a secret. Frances entered the room and crossed to him quickly, taking a seat at his side.

"Good morning, Brother," she said too cheerfully.

He only scowled back.

"How is the jam this morning? Worth the trouble?"

"I want to speak to you." Ezra stood, taking Frances's hand and pulling her to her feet.

"Well, excellent, because I have some splendid ideas on what we can do between now and the ball tonight." She chatted the entire way to the door. "I would hate to grow bored with nothing to do all day."

They rounded the corner and Ezra glanced around them. No one else was in sight.

He turned back to his sister. "What are you doing here?"

Her eyes went wide, but her attempt at innocence was wasted on him. "I'm getting breakfast."

"Frances," he warned.

She folded her arms, her expression instantly morphing into one of annoyance. "Katherine wrote to me. Informed me that you were carrying on with that girl from the country."

Blasted letters. It was letters that had gotten him into this mess in the first place. Now, it was a letter that was making everything worse.

"She's not 'that girl from the country.' She's a beautiful young lady. One I happen to find immensely attractive and everything a lady ought to be."

Frances shrugged with one shoulder. "I told you not to isolate yourself so during the Season. Now you can't see the difference between quality and . . . *that*."

"You will speak of her with respect."

Frances listed her head. "Has she bewitched you so completely?"

Yes, most certainly. All thanks to Frances's immature refusal to respond to a letter five months ago. But he wasn't ready to admit quite so much to his sister. He needed to speak with Grace first. He wanted things settled between them before he spoke out of turn and yet again risked losing all.

"If you were truly a woman of good breeding," he said, "you would show every person respect, no matter their station."

Frances's nose wrinkled. "Not according to my governess." She pushed past him and strode back into the breakfast room.

Ezra stayed out in the corridor, listening to the sounds of voices and the occasional bit of laughter. He recognized Grace's voice once then twice among the din but couldn't make out exactly what she was saying.

He stood there, wholly unsure what to do. He wanted, more than anything, to go back into the breakfast room and sit beside Grace.

See if there wasn't some way they could find the ease and friendship that they'd shared so readily this holiday season. Part of him didn't dare. He'd seen already that his presence was not wanted, that she had no desire to speak with him or even look at him.

Eventually, people started leaving the room. Grace was among them, walking beside Lady Augusta. She wasn't smiling as he moved up beside her.

"May I have a word?" he asked in a low tone.

Lady Augusta looked to Grace, silently asking if she wished to be left alone with him.

It hurt that whether Grace would care to speak to him was an uncertainty.

Grace glanced up at him, then turned back to Lady Augusta and gave her a nod.

Lady Augusta moved away and down the corridor.

Ezra waited until they were alone before speaking. Still he kept his voice soft. "I feel I need to apologize again."

She spared him only a passing glance. "Do you?"

"You are clearly upset."

"Of course I'm upset." For the first time that morning, a bit of sincerity etched its way into her tone.

"Perhaps if I explain again—"

"No." She held a hand up and stepped back and away from him. "I need some time to think this over."

He didn't want her to leave, not still angry or confused because of him. Lud, it burned, this knowledge that he'd caused her pain.

However, if she needed time and space to think, he would respect that. "Will I see you at the ball tonight?"

Her impassive expression was back firmly in place. "I don't know."

With that, she turned and left him standing alone in the corridor.

Grace spent the rest of the day in her room. She hadn't brought all of "Frances's" letters from home with her. But she had brought a few of the more recent ones. London Season had proved to be overwhelming and lonely, and she had rather feared that this holiday house party may prove the same. So she'd packed a few letters in case she found she needed the connection and reassurance they always provided. She'd not known then how much she'd need to read them over again now.

Did it pour in Cavershire like it did here in London last week? We were shut away for several days, and I found myself thinking of our previous conversation regarding Byron and his words: "And storm, and darkness, ye are wondrous strong." There truly is a most magnificent strength to a fierce storm, one I cannot help but be inspired by.

She'd fully believed they'd been Frances's words when she'd first read them. Now, reading over them again, she could only hear them in Ezra's voice.

Mother was ill again today. I have sent for the doctor, and he assures me she will soon be well and that it is nothing serious. But there are moments I look over and all I can see is the white in her hair, the wrinkles around her eyes, and the years that seem to hang from her shoulders, dragging her down. I have tried to be a support and a comfort to her, but I fear there is much I will never be able to do. Though she speaks of him infrequently, I know she misses my father most terribly.

Grace read the familiar lines, seeing them in a wholly new light now. The evening wore on, and soon she had to light a candle beside her to keep reading. To either side of her room, she could hear the bustling and excited tones of the other ladies getting ready. Her own mother had come to check on her a few times throughout the day, but Grace had simply said she wasn't feeling up to socializing now. Eventually, her maid had come to help her get ready, but Grace had asked for a few more minutes alone.

She'd been so looking forward to tonight's ball, but now she felt certain she wouldn't be able to enjoy herself, even if she did attend. She was much too confused; she had no idea what to think about the letters and all Ezra had told her.

A soft noise caused her to turn her head. A small slip of white rested on the floor near her bedchamber door.

Another letter.

She walked over to it and picked it up. It wasn't sealed as the Ezra's other letters had been, but it was clearly his handwriting scrawled across the front. Grace tapped it gently against a hand as she moved back to her desk. She placed it atop the others but didn't open it.

He'd written her again.

But is that what she wanted? More written words?

In a way, yes. She loathed the idea of losing the companionship she'd found in Ezra's letters. They'd developed a friendship that had become paramount in her life.

But now?

Now it could never be the same.

She didn't want it to be, if she were being honest with herself. What she and Ezra had had before wasn't enough.

But with the lies heavy between them, what chance did they have of building something more?

FOURTEEN

EZRA LOOKED OVER THE ballroom. When he'd left Bridgecross Manor, he'd asked after Grace and her parents, none of whom where in the entryway ready to depart with the rest of them. Lady Augusta had informed him that they only needed a few more minutes and would follow behind shortly.

That had been nearly two hours ago, and though he stayed near the ballroom door so as not to miss any newcomer, he'd yet to see any of the Stewarts. It was uncharacteristically rude of him, but he'd yet to stand up with anyone so far. He didn't dare step away from his post. No doubt, the moment he did would be the moment Grace would decide to arrive, and he would miss her.

First Frances, then Lady Katherine, then his sister once more had tried to persuade him to dance or get some mulled cider, or even step outside to accompany them as they cooled themselves for a moment. But he'd refused each time. He needed to talk to Grace. At the very least he needed to ascertain if she'd given up on him for good. If not, then he would wait as long as she needed, though he couldn't exactly promise not to continue pleading his case.

If she had . . . well, then he still couldn't promise he wouldn't stay nearby and plead his case.

Devil take him, but he was a hopeless cause.

She stepped into the room.

Ezra drew himself up, instantly stepping toward her. She was resplendent in a soft rose-colored dress. Her hair was piled atop her head with several curls framing her face. She turned his way as he drew near.

For all her beauty, her smile was still forced. No matter what she wore or how her hair was done, nothing could replace the joy that used to shine through every time she looked at him. Heaven help him, what he wouldn't give to see that joy again.

"Good evening, Mr. Stewart, Mrs. Stewart." He turned toward Grace fully. "Miss Stewart."

They all bowed, and her parents bid him good evening.

"It is rather warm in here, isn't it?" Grace asked. Even her words were flat and quite unlike the cheerful tones he had grown used to hearing from her.

"Yes," he hurried to say. "Would you join me in a turn about the back of the room? The doors are cracked open there, and it is a bit cooler."

Her parents allowed Grace to leave on his arm. They circled about the ballroom, keeping close to the wall. Her hand was stiff against his arm, much as it had been ever since he had told her the truth.

Finally, they reached the back of the room. A trickle of winter air slipped in through a window cracked slightly open. Grace let go of him and folded her arms, facing the door completely. Her reflection against the glass told him she wasn't smiling.

"You have very elegant handwriting," she said softly enough that only he would hear.

Ezra chuckled softly. Relief that she was willing to talk to him about this eased some of the weight pressing against his chest. "Of all the compliments I've ever been given in a ballroom, I can't say that is one of them."

The tips of Grace's lips pulled up somewhat. "I don't suppose it would have been."

Ezra shifted his weight. "Did you read my last letter then?"

"No."

Instantly, all the relief he'd felt before vanished.

Grace turned and faced him, holding out the small bit of white foolscap he'd slipped beneath her door earlier that day. "I'm tired of letters, Ezra. If you have something to say, I need to you say it to me directly."

He couldn't deny that Grace had a point. Ezra reached out and took the unread letter, slipping it back in his pocket before anyone might see.

"Letters are what started this between us," he said by way of explanation. "I was hoping it might be letters that could bring us back together once more."

Grace shook her head. "We cannot solve a problem by continuing in the same manner that caused it originally."

Ezra smiled softly. "Well said." He glanced over his shoulder at the swirling couples in the center of the ballroom. "This isn't exactly the place for a private conversation."

"The corridor just outside?" she offered.

Ezra moved closer, close enough to smell the rose water on her, and placed a hand at the small of her back as he gently led her through a set of double doors on the far side of the ballroom. The corridor was far less packed with people. With a quick glance around to make sure they wouldn't be seen, they slipped down an adjoining hallway and away from the bustle and crowd.

Once they were apart from all the others, Ezra felt himself ease. "Is this better?"

Grace had her face tipped upward as she studied him closely. "You truly do not like crowds, do you?"

"You should have heard some of the embarrassing things I said in the past." He turned so that his back was pressed up against the wall. "Being among so many people mucks up my brain. My words come out all wrong."

Grace moved up close to him, pressing her back against the wall beside him.

How comfortable it was, standing here with her. As though they'd always known one another. As though there was nothing more natural in all the world than standing beside her, speaking whatever was on his mind.

If only he could be sure this wouldn't be the last time.

"Grace," he began, his tone carrying the weight he felt. "I never lied to you."

"You mean, other than leading me to believe you were your own sister?"

True, there had been that. "Other than signing my name as Frances instead of Ezra, yes, I never told you a single thing that wasn't true."

Grace seemed to mull that over for a minute. Finally she said, "I guess I had rather wondered why a lady who I remembered as being perfectly elegant and polite would write that she had no great love for embroidery or playing music. But that she rather preferred a bruising ride along the countryside."

Ezra smiled. "I remember writing that particular letter. I was more than a little worried you would figure me out."

Grace turned, pressing her shoulder against the wall instead of her back, and faced him fully. "Then why did you? Why did you keep writing?"

Her hand dangled temptingly close to his own. "Because each letter was just like your first. You spoke the words in my own heart." Ezra reached out, brushing his fingertips against hers. "I kept writing because I wanted to. Because I wanted to know you better. Because I wanted you to know me."

Her eyes took on that thoughtful gaze he'd come to know so well. It wasn't the warm spark he was hoping for, but it was far better than the cold, hurt look he'd seen so much as of late.

"I feel mortified," she said barely above a whisper. "I never would have written so many of those things if . . ."

If she'd been aware of the truth. "I know. And that's why I kept writing as Frances. I knew you would close off if you found yourself writing to a gentleman. I didn't want that." He wrapped his fingers firmly around hers, taking her hand fully. She didn't pull away, and he counted that as a reason to hope. "I wanted the real you."

She cast her gaze heavenward. "And then that stupid letter all about Lord Brown."

"Whatever else you think or say, never regret that one."

The confusion returned to her expression. Clearly, she had no idea how much that particular letter had affected him.

"It was that letter," Ezra continued, "that made me realize that letters alone weren't enough for me any longer." Ezra pulled in a deep breath and all the courage he could muster. "It made me realize how much I'd come to love you."

Her eyes went wide. "You what?"

"With every letter, every thought shared, I fell in love with you. I was already a lost cause before we ever formally met at Bridgecross Manor."

Grace rocked back, releasing his hand and bringing both of hers up to her face. "My goodness."

Ezra pressed off the wall. "Grace, I'm sorry there was need to deceive you. I'm sorry we couldn't have become friends on more even grounds. But I am not sorry I wrote you that first letter, and I'm not sorry I continued to write. If I hadn't, I never would have gotten to know you as I have. I never would have seen what a brilliant and kind-hearted lady you are. I never would have found in you my equal in mind and conviction. For all that, I cannot be sorry."

Her hands slipped down. "You truly love me?"

The optimism in her voice nearly undid him. Ezra closed the distance between them, wrapping his arms completely around her. "Hopelessly so. Completely and entirely."

Her eyes lit up, the joy he'd been wishing to see filling them completely. "I have to confess, it's taken me some time to reconcile the person I thought I was writing with the person I've come to know in you. If I'm being completely honest, I was already half-way to being in love with you before I learned you and my correspondent were one and the same."

"And now?" He leaned forward, resting his forehead against hers.

"Now I think I might be as hopelessly in love with you as you are with me."

"Completely and entirely in love?"

Her hands snaked around his neck. "Completely and entirely."

His lips met hers in a kiss that burned away all the uncertainty of before. All that was hidden was now known, and all that had been cherished was now all the more precious. She pulled him in closer still, and for several minutes, there were no thoughts of sisters, or letters, or anything beyond the two of them and that single kiss that blended into a second and then a third.

After a time—Ezra had quite lost track of how long—they pulled away slightly.

"Marry me, dearest?" he asked, his mouth trailing kisses across her jaw and over the soft spot beneath her ear.

"I suppose I shall have to now."

He chuckled. "Now that I have kissed you scandalously?"

"Now that you have given me no choice but to love you in return."

And that, Ezra felt, was excuse enough to kiss her again.

EPILOGUE

THREE DAYS LATER

Lady Augusta chose to sit in a small chair beside the fire instead of the settee, which would normally have been the first place she would have wished to sit. The benefit to picking the settee was simply that it allowed another person—a gentleman if she were lucky—to sit beside her.

But tonight, she far preferred sitting alone.

In one corner of the parlor, Grace and Lord Weston sat close to one another, deep in a hushed conversation. Grace had explained everything to Augusta regarding the correspondence she'd believed she was sharing with Lady Frances, only to learn it was actually Lord Weston she'd been writing to all this time. Though Augusta didn't know of what they spoke, she caught their smiles and their soft laughter and was happy for them. At least one engagement had come from this holiday house party. Her gaze caught on Lady Katherine and Lady Frances sitting together in another corner, casting angry scowls at anyone who neared them. The irony there was that Lady Katherine had wanted Lord Brown so long as he had been bent on pursuing Grace. But when Grace and Lord Weston had announced their engagement the day after the Twelfth Night ball, a littleness in both Lady Katherine and Lady Frances had been made quite well known to everyone present. The gentlemen had been steering clear of either lady since.

Augusta shook her head sadly and turned back toward the fire. It never ended well when one belittled another. It was a lesson her mother had instilled in her as a young girl—one that was proving far harder to follow now than Augusta had ever imagined. What her elder sister chose did not sit well with Augusta, yet she was trying to be a supportive sister all the same. Never mind that it had shamed the family and ended Augusta's first London Season early.

But the more and more she found herself pushed slightly to the outskirts of society, the harder and harder it was becoming for her to keep her head up and stay loving toward her sister and optimistic regarding her own future.

Her mind drifted back to Mother's words that morning. Now, more ruin was besetting them. First, her sister's scandalous elopement with an undergardener, and now Father's most recent speculation was rumored to have been fully lost.

Grace would be leaving this house party with hope and a brilliant future, sure to be full of love and joy.

But Augusta—she would be leaving worse off than when she'd first arrived.

So much for Christmas cheer.

Augusta stood and slowly moved toward the door. Since they would be leaving first thing in the morning, she might as well get a good night's sleep first.

A hand on her arm stopped her just before she walked out of the parlor completely.

"Are you well?" Grace asked her.

Tears at her new friend's gentle question blurred Augusta's sight. "Just tired. It's been a rather exciting Christmas, hasn't it?"

Grace nodded, and though she was clearly trying to contain herself, Augusta didn't miss the way her eyes danced or the loving glance she cast over her shoulder toward Lord Weston.

Augusta patted Grace's arm. "You two are perfect for one another."

"We are," she agreed. "I never would have guessed it had we met in London earlier this year. But I am so glad to have found him now."

"Promise me," Augusta said, "that you will appreciate what you two have. That you won't risk it for anything."

Grace's smile dropped. "Now I am truly concerned."

Augusta shook her head. She'd spoken too forcibly. "Forgive me. Only, I know not every woman is granted the Christmas gift you got this year."

Herself, for example. Only earlier that year, Augusta had been a much sought-after debutante. Young, but highly desirable when seen through a prudential light. Now, her family name was tainted by scandal, and her father's wealth was hanging in the balance. What once had been a sure thing—marriage to a man of her own choosing, a life of comfort and love—was no longer a guarantee.

"I am truly blessed," Grace agreed, but her worry for Augusta was still evident.

Augusta spread her arms and wrapped her friend in a hug. "Do not worry about me. All will be well, I promise." Augusta only said those words to buoy herself up. She had no promise at all that things would be well. But neither could she fix them.

So where did that leave her?

Focused on being happy for her friend, and focused on making the most of her situation, whatever that might look like in another few months.

She felt utterly lost, but she wasn't going to let that drive her into despair.

"I leave in the morning," Augusta said, pulling back once more. "Promise me you shall write?" Life was easier with good friends.

Grace nodded. "I have become quite good at making friends through letters this year."

Augusta laughed. If only she had a secret correspondence she could turn to now. At least she could count on Grace, and she had other friends who would not leave her side.

"I shall miss you." Augusta gave Grace another quick hug and then bid her good night and hurried toward the door.

She peaked over her shoulder briefly before leaving the parlor, catching one last look at a smitten Lord Weston and a joyfully happy Grace Stewart.

Christmas could indeed be a time of miracles.

She could only hope that someday, it would prove to be the same for her.

The End

The romance continues with
Lady Augusta's story in
Sugar Plums and Scandal

FREE DOWNLOAD

**He's been waiting months for her
to finally notice him.**

**Except suddenly, he's not the only one
vying for her hand.**

Download the short story for free at:
www.LauraRollins.com

ACKNOWEDGMENTS

No book is ever written without a lot of love and support from many, many people. I could not even begin to list them all, but I will name a few of those who have made the biggest difference, and have been my proudest cheerleaders.

First, I want to thank all my writer friends; those in ANWA, those I've met along the way, and certainly my Obstinate Headstrong ladies. Your encouragement and understanding of what being an author is like has made a huge difference in my life. You have inspired me, taught me, and loved me through all the ups and downs of publishing.

Next, a big shout out to my family. To my kids--thank you for understanding when I say I need to write. Thank you for being patient with fast dinners and for doing a load of dishes when asked. To my husband--I cannot say thank you enough for always encouraging me and supporting me. The muse may take me all sorts of random directions, but knowing you've always got my back makes everything possible.

Lastly, thanks to my Heavenly Father, for giving me a beautiful life and the opportunity to create.

ABOUT THE AUTHOR

 Laura Rollins has always loved a heart-melting happily ever after. It didn't matter if the story took place in Regency England, or in a cobbler's shop, if there was a sweet romance, she would read it.

Life has given her many of her own adventures. Currently, she lives in the Rocky Mountains with her best friend, who is also her husband, and their four beautiful children. She still loves to read books, books, and more books; her favorite types of music are classical, Broadway, and country; she loves hiking in the mountains near her home; and she's been known to debate with her oldest son about whether Infinity is better categorized as a number or an idea.

You can learn more about her and her books, as well as pick up a free story, at:
www.LauraRollins.com